OUR FIRST NOEL

HEATHER CAMACHO

RENEWED HEARTS | BOOK ONE POINT FIVE

"Heather Camacho has a beautiful way with words. I was immediately drawn into her debut novel from the very beginning. She is a talented storyteller, and her books are guaranteed to take any reader on an emotional adventure."

— MANDI BLAKE, USA TODAY BESTSELLING
AUTHOR OF THE LOVE IN BLACKWATER SERIES

"Heather Camacho has a way with words that bring fictional people to life, drawing readers in to relatable stories of faith and the challenges real people face every day. If Heather's name is on the cover, I wouldn't hesitate for a moment to pick up her book."

— MISSY KAMPA, CO-AUTHOR OF THE ALTERRIAN
GIFTS TRILOGY

"Heather is a brilliant writer! She has a gift for pulling you into her stories and keeping you there. It's easy to fall in love with the characters in the story and leave you wanting more!"

— PHILIP REED, AUTHOR OF BY THE BLOOD

"Heather is a very gifted and captivating writer. Her story-lines, suspense, and creativity, keep me engaged from beginning to end... Bravo!!!"

— DEBBIE LYNNE HENDERSON, AUTHOR OF THE
NONSENSE AND RHYME CHILDREN'S COLLECTION

OUR FIRST NOEL

HEATHER CAMACHO

ALSO BY HEATHER CAMACHO

RENEWED HEARTS

(Novels)

From Graves to Gardens

From Mourning to Dancing

(Novellas)

Our First Noel

ANTHOLOGIES

The Magic of Us

For Alyssa Espinoza — For waiting until after I hit the "confirm" button on my author copy order to tell me she found a typo. And then following it up with "Just kidding." Or, for keeping the same email address for over 14 years. That's pretty impressive. Oh, and also for agreeing to proofread this story at the literal last minute. Not many would drop everything to do that. You're an absolute gem of a friend.

For Kass — The best farrier ever to exist. You have come through for me and my horses like nobody else, and I'll never cease to be grateful.

For God — The only reason I was able to bring this story from conception to completion in a matter of weeks. How You always speak up if we just quiet down and listen. Thank you!

SARAH

1

My little blue Corolla couldn't get me home fast enough. December had come and the last of finals had ended, and now I had the rest of winter break ahead of me. I was heading back to Corpus Christi from the university in Killeen, and I was more than ready to see the faces of all my favorite people.

Thanksgiving was the last time I saw my parents, when they brought Kevin and Marie up to surprise me for the weekend. And I hadn't seen my friends since well before that when I left for school in the fall. I had come home to see Kevin in October after his release, but only for a couple of days. It was all the time I could afford to spare from class, and I had to more than make up for it, but it was extra credit well spent.

Technically, I had just seen Kevin two hours ago, when we hung up FaceTime so I could start my drive. And, yeah, even though we did the video chat thing regularly, I *still* missed him. Because of that, I would make the most of our time together, no matter what.

No matter what?

Suppressing the lump in my throat, I steeled myself. Dwelling on things I couldn't change right now wouldn't serve me, and it wouldn't bring joy to our reunion. For the time being, I had to focus on the positive, even if that meant temporarily ignoring the inconvenient truth.

After the long six months he spent in juvie, with the request that I focus on myself, I already knew what being without him was like. I didn't care for it, so I was all too eager to keep him as close as I could, whenever I could. I didn't need less of him to have more of me. Life felt like a perfect blend of us both, and I was exceedingly happy. We both were.

A little over two hours to go and I would be back in his arms, home again, greeted by the breezy coastal town that never forgets you and the friends and family that will love you forever.

On the radio, everyone was talking about the same thing. The hot topic as of late was the fact that South Texas wasn't very hot at all that winter. Rumor was it might even snow. *Pfft. Yeah, right.*

Many current residents had never seen a white Christmas in the coastal bend, and I didn't see why that year wouldn't be any different. Regardless if my breath perfectly ghosted out in front of my face when I exhaled.

Pulling into Corpus, I was indeed greeted by the cool breeze of winter. The sea winds tickled my senses as they sailed through my cracked window, over my skin, welcoming me home with its familiarity. I wished there was a way to bring more of home to school with me every time I went back. Something to make the homesickness a little more tolerable.

I slowed down around the curve leading to my street and saw him right away. Standing on the sidewalk at the edge of my lawn, Kevin was waving, smiling brightly at me.

My heart burst with joy. "Thank you, God, for bringing me

home safely, and for all the welcome arms to greet me. Thank you, thank you."

Coming to a stop in the driveway behind my mom's car, I was on autopilot as I watched Kevin hurry over. He had my door open before I could kill the engine and get the seat belt off. Once I was free, I allowed his brawny arms to hoist me out and cradle me securely in the best Welcome Home hug. My toes dangled over the concrete driveway.

"Is it just me, or was that the longest month ever?"

"It's not just you." He pulled back to kiss my forehead. My bangs, which I had recently cut at the late-night urging of my roommate, had grown out to the point of being able to swipe to both sides. He brushed the right cluster behind my ear. "I don't know how much longer I can stand saying goodbye to you."

"Are you still going to apply for the spring semester?"

Rather than immediately agreeing, his smile dipped into something else, raising my curiosity. Had his plans for school changed? What reason would he have for doing that? Perhaps he had his own unpleasant news to share.

"I'm still planning on it," was all he had time to say. Then, my parents, who had graciously given us our first moments alone, had come bursting through the front door for their turn.

KEVIN

2

SARAH AND I WERE LYING IN THE HAMMOCK IN HER BACKYARD, gently swaying back and forth. As the evening was coming to an end, my mind went to the folded piece of paper in my pocket. The plan was to leave her with it as a parting gift when I went home, but I just wasn't ready to go yet. In my pocket it stayed, for just a little while longer.

There was a lot of pressure on that piece of paper. It had to properly convey to Sarah all the things I couldn't afford to say with conventional gifts. The depths of my feelings for her couldn't be bought, but it sure would've been nice to have something other than a to-do list written on a piece of scrap to give her for our first Christmas together.

Some part of me also worried that she wouldn't like it as much as I hoped she would. Maybe she'd think I was being too cheesy. Or, maybe it would be just cheesy enough. It was difficult being away from each other for long periods of time, because little doubts like that crept up easier than they would otherwise.

Having her back in town always restored a missing piece of my heart that only Sarah could. We had been separated for longer, and under more extreme circumstances, but two days or two months, it all felt the same. Watching her fade into the distance every time we had to separate was torture. I knew it was only temporary and reuniting was always worth it, but the time between proved difficult anyway.

"What do you want for Christmas?" Sarah asked me, her gaze lingering skyward through the swaying trees.

"Nothing." The only thing I felt like I needed couldn't be given to me by her. Like another free ride to college, or at the very least, an easier one. There were options, even for people with a colorful history like mine, but I felt the weight of the mounting pressure regarding school finances more every day.

"Everyone wants something."

I shrugged. "All I want is you."

"You already have me. Pick something I can give you."

Perhaps the best way to combat her relentlessness was with a dose of my own. There was something I hadn't tried in a while. "Okay, fine. How about you give me forever?"

She turned and looked at me, a suspicious smile turning up the corners of her mouth. "Are you trying to propose again?"

"Maybe. Are you saying yes this time?" I dared not think it was possible.

"You know we aren't old enough."

"Not old enough to rent a car, either," I muttered behind my smile. We'd had a similar conversation before, and she laughed when she recognized it. "But if you ask me, we're plenty old enough to love each other unconditionally until death-do-us-part." I already did.

"You're ridiculous," she declared playfully, with a shake of her head. A few rays of remaining sun snuck their way into the yard above the wooden fence, glinting off her light strawberry locks, holding me captive. She looked up again, watching the leaves move to and fro, with a look of pleased serenity on her face.

It wasn't an actual proposal; we both knew that. And even if it was, I knew she wouldn't accept like this — nor would I expect her to — but my silly heart had still gone irregular on me. One of these days, I would ask that question for real and receive a proper answer. And there was only one answer I could imagine getting…

God, how did I ever live without her?

"Anyway, back to Christmas," Sarah insisted. "Here's the deal, Kevin. I'm going to get you something regardless, so you might as well tell me what you could use or would like. I've always been really bad at gift-giving, and if you don't help me out, I could end up buying you a really butt-ugly sweater or something."

"Your husband would wear anything you gave him, butt-ugly or not. I'm just saying."

"Ha-ha." She rolled her eyes but couldn't hide the humor inside them.

"Okay, you win, but just for now. I'm not giving up," I conceded, at least until the next time. "But you don't have to buy me anything. It just so happens, I actually have something for you, and I think it could work well as a gift for us both."

"Really? What is it?"

I reached into the pocket of my jeans and grasped the folded piece of paper. *Here goes nothing.*

SARAH

3

"'Our First Christmas To-Do List?'" My happiness grew to almost more than my heart could handle. The piece of paper Kevin handed me was well-creased with blue tint where his jeans had stained the edges. Evidence of having spent a lot of time in his pocket. It warmed my heart to see him so sentimental. "You really want to do all these things?"

"Yeah." He rubbed the back of his neck. "Do you think it's dumb?"

"No way!" I shot upright in the hammock. He laughed as we rode the shockwave of my exclamation. "This is the sweetest thing I've ever seen. I can't wait to do all these things with you, Kevin. This is a better gift than anything I could've possibly imagined."

"Is it better than a butt-ugly sweater?"

"It's a hard sell when you put it that way, but yes," I winked. "So when can we get started?"

His eyes lit up. "Anytime. Right now?"

"Don't you have to leave soon, though?"

"Maybe you could come with me. We can do number one and

I'll take you home after. You can bring your parents a batch of freshly baked cookies."

I pondered it for a moment. "Do you have all the ingredients already?"

"Yeah, I do. I made sure the kitchen was stocked before you got home. Well, my mom did, specifically."

"Do you even know how to bake?"

"Not really, but I know how to print and read a recipe. If nothing else, I can just stand in the corner and look cute while you do all the baking." Kevin folded his hand adorably under his chin and batted his dark brown eyes, earning himself a giddy slap on the wrist.

"Not a chance, Betty Crocker. We're doing this together." I leaned up and threw my legs over the hammock's edge. "Let's run inside and clear it with my parents first."

Kevin stood up and reached for my hand. "Let's do it."

SARAH

4

1. Bake Cookies

I TILTED MY HEAD, INSPECTING WHAT WAS SUPPOSED TO BE A FRESH batch of cinnamon snickerdoodle cookie batter. "Are you *sure* you know how to read a recipe?" Lifting the whisk, I watched the lumpy liquid fall in sad drips and plop into the bowl on my arm.

Kevin threw his face into his hand, and his elbows landed on the counter. "I give up."

Pulling the recipe back out, it was already covered in crust and splatters. So was the counter. It would seem that *neither* of us could read a recipe. I scanned down the list for areas where we could've gone wrong. There were many. "Did you under-measure the baking soda, maybe?"

"I don't know. Is that what makes it thick?"

"I really have no idea. You know, I used to always think I was smart, but this stuff has made me question everything I know. Baking is no joke."

"I think we should just go buy cookies instead. It's a lot safer."

Determined, I set the bowl on the counter with a thud. "Abso-

9

lutely not! We are going to best this recipe; it will not best us. Besides, when the cookies are done, they're going to taste amazing because they were made with love and good frickin cheer!" Kevin's shoulders bounced with his laughter. I wasn't sure if that meant my speech was convincing or not. "What is so funny?"

"You seem really worked up over cookies."

"So, why is that funny?"

"I just think you could chill out a little."

Taking a deep breath, I pinned him with a glare. "Has that advice ever worked for any female in the history of ever?"

With a devious smile, Kevin grabbed a spatula from the counter, dipped it into the batter, and with one hand, pulled it back like a catapult.

"Don't you d — " *SPLAT.* Suddenly, my face was a runny, sugary mess. Using both hands, I wiped my eyes free of the cookie goop. As I blinked up at Kevin, his jovial form came into focus. "You did not just do that."

All the while, he clutched his middle to comfort the ache as he laughed on. "You didn't sound too cheerful to me. Now you do!"

"You want cheer?" I fake-laughed at a decibel that matched Kevin's, and with all my might, flicked my hands clean by flinging them at him.

Rather than put him in his place, his eyes went wide. He tasted the batter on his lips and nodded. "Hmm. It's actually not that bad. But I do think we forgot the cinnamon."

"Oh, let me get it." I reached under the cabinet to where the bottle of cinnamon had been hiding, and sure enough, it was still sealed. "Looks like you're right," I said, peeling it open. Then, hoping to sweeten my revenge — literally — I pulled open his shirt and dumped the entire bottle.

Acting quickly, he jumped out of the way and billowed his shirt, letting most of the russet-hued powder scatter to the floor. "You're on, Stevenson!" came his battle-cry.

It was an all-out war at that point. Batter, baking soda, sugar, and cinnamon all went flying. We scooped the batter up by the hand and smashed it into each other's clothes and faces, laughter and ingredients filling the kitchen. Kevin was right. *This* was good cheer.

Before I knew it, Kevin had gained the upper hand. In his palm, he smugly showed off a large brown egg.

I gasped. "Where did that come from?"

"A magician never reveals his secrets."

I didn't stick around to inquire further. I simply ran. There wasn't far to go, but I managed a few laps around the island and through the living room before he jumped over the sofa and tackled me. Upon impact, the egg in his hand — and the second one hiding in his pocket — both smashed.

The one in his hand made contact with the top of my head and dripped down the sides of my face. I gathered as much as I could and returned the favor, giving him a delightful new hairstyle, until we were equally coated in the gelatinous gunk.

Home with her son for the weekend, Marie chose that moment to emerge from her room to investigate the ruckus. We looked up from the floor like two startled raccoons in the trash, and when she took it all in, she busted up and turned around. "Never mind. I don't actually need anything right now. I'm staying out of this. But these better be some fantastic cookies!" We heard the door close behind her and burst into another fit of laughter.

I thought I might never catch my breath again until Kevin took the inside of his wrist and wiped my mouth clean. The moment quieted. We looked at each other and I smiled. He kissed me then, slowly, yet in such a way that made it hard to breathe all over again.

I pulled back with a giggle, smacking my lips. The batter was still front and center. "You're right. We definitely forgot the cinnamon." He stood up and helped me to my feet.

"I'm pretty sure we have enough ingredients to start over, and the oven is still preheated. Let's give it one more shot before you have to leave."

"Great idea. Truce?"

Smirking, he agreed, "Truce."

In the next hour, we redid the batter, baked the cookies, and began cleaning the kitchen. By the time the cinnamon treats were fragrant and cooled on the rack, Marie came back out.

"I really wasn't sure if you guys were gonna be able to do it, but those smell amazing. Are they ready yet?"

"Just about, but we're finishing the cleaning first."

Marie stepped into the kitchen, not bothering to bypass the remaining splatters on the floor. "You guys don't worry about the rest of that. I'll get it."

"No way, Mom. We made it, we'll clean it."

"It's okay. Joyful messes are easier to deal with. Just leave me a couple of those cookies, if you don't mind."

"Are you sure?"

"Yes, Kevin. Go ahead and take her home. Don't worry about all this."

Kevin gave his mom a big hug, knowing full well that he would leave her covered in our first batch of batter. She swatted after him when he kissed her cheek, but her face was pleased. Grabbing his keys, Kevin threw his arm around my shoulder. "Thanks, Mom. I'll be right back."

"Drive safely, son," Marie called.

"I will."

I waved before we were out the door. "Goodnight, Marie. See you later."

She smiled back. "Goodnight, Sarah."

My heart was full and my hands were warm as I held the container of cookies, minus four for Marie, in my lap. I rested my head on Kevin's shoulder as he drove me back to my parents' house.

Images of a life with him in our own cozy home, making memories just like we had that night, gleamed like a shooting star in my mind. The two of us laughing together, playing and cooking terribly every single day for the rest of forever seemed like something so tangible and right. Getting dirty wouldn't matter. Messing up wouldn't matter.

It wouldn't always be *that* fun to get messy; I knew that much for sure. But we had each other. I didn't doubt we'd get through anything we faced.

KEVIN

5

MOM WAS SITTING AT THE ISLAND EATING THE COOKIES WHEN I got home. The kitchen was now spotless, completely void of any evidence of our baking catastrophe.

I tossed my keys on the counter. "I'm sorry again for leaving the mess, but wow. Looks great in here."

Her jaw was working on her latest bite. "Don't be sorry. It made me happy to hear you two having so much fun. I want that kind of amusement in this poor old house."

I knew exactly how she felt about that. It was such a drastic change that the only things happening around here now were good. A little more each day, spending time with Sarah was like fulfilling a childhood dream. It made itself present in the simple things as well as the big.

Such as the list I made for Sarah. That was my very simple way of giving her something special, without being able to give her much at all. The savings account of a guy on probation post-release was not great, and I still had tuition and all the other school-related costs to worry about. Plus, living away from home came with a slew of additional expenses.

Always something. There would *always* be something with the potential to hold me back, but I'd gained a lot of healthy perspective on things over the year. I was more positive than I would've been before everything happened, but the reality was, I needed more money than I currently had.

Money. Said to be the root of all evil, and the original cause of why I'd gotten into such major trouble to begin with. At least there was no way I'd go down a road like that ever again, no matter how desperate things got.

My mom's crunching drew me back to the moment. "Well, thank you, for all this."

"You're welcome, but these babies are thanks enough." She held up the remaining bite of the cookie in her hand.

"Oh, nice. So, they taste good?"

She turned on her stool and looked me square in the face. "They taste absolutely terrible, son."

"You gotta be kidding me. After all that work? There's no way. Let me try it." I reached, and she delivered. The outside was like a hockey puck, while the softness on the inside was deceptively pleasant. It had a decent flavor, but the moment the chewy morsel went around my mouth, I knew she was right.

Despite my desire not to, I choked the whole thing down. If nothing else, I needed to show support for what Sarah and I had haphazardly created. "Disgusting. At least they were really fun to make."

"I'll say. I love seeing you so happy, kid. I know you have a harder time when Sarah is gone. You're not quite like this when you miss her."

I gave her a halfhearted smile. She'd struck a bit of a nerve, but she wasn't quite correct about why. "I'll be honest, that isn't only because I miss her."

She watched me. "What is it about then?"

The answer wasn't so romantic. "School."

"What do you mean, school? Are you jealous she's there without you?"

"No, I'm not jealous. I'm very proud of Sarah and what she's doing. My worry is that I won't be able to go, too. I'm pretty sure I'll be accepted, but how will I pay for it?"

"Haven't you turned in your financial aid paperwork and all that?"

"Yeah, but you never know. And I have a unique setback that most of their other applicants don't. I'm just… really trying to enjoy Sarah's vacation with her as much as I can, without letting the stress come in. It's hard sometimes."

"I agree with that approach. Don't worry about it right now, son. We'll get it all figured out." My mom's hand came to a solid rest on my shoulder. "What you can't get in grants or scholarships, we'll simply make up for. I am working full-time now, you know, so I am going to be helping you. And don't forget we're renting the house out during the school year."

"Mom, you're going to need that money, too. You can't be giving it to me."

"I don't recall asking your permission." Her mom-tone was more than a mom-tone; it was a Marie tone, and there was no arguing with it.

I sighed, hanging my head. "I know. Thanks, Mom." Of course, I appreciated her help. She was my mom, after all. But I didn't want to *need* help from anyone. Old habits really died hard. But even with the assistance and my mom's help, it wouldn't cover everything required. Tuition was just the tip of the iceberg when everyday living expenses were factored in.

Since I'd lost my scholarship earlier in the year, getting into college was only going to happen by the skin of my teeth. I hated dragging my mom into it, but at the same time, deep down, it felt nice that she was doing motherly things like that. God had been so good to us both, and I knew His plans for me entailed getting out for a while, even if things at home had drastically improved.

One way or another, I was determined to make things happen. In the meantime, I was forcing myself to stay more concerned with giving Sarah a great Christmas, despite my limited means. As long as she had a special time, then that's what I wanted. So far, I was getting my wish.

SARAH

6

KEVIN ARRIVED TO TAKE ME TO BREAKFAST AND I HOPPED DOWN the driveway to his truck. It was a cool, crisp morning, with a velvety blanket sky over head. We had plans with Tyler and Cindie later, but not until tonight, once it was nice and dark.

I bid Kevin good morning with a kiss, but something important looked to be turning over in his mind. "Is everything okay?"

He reached for my door handle and held onto it, rather than pull it open. His eyes were sad. "Would you mind if we changed our daytime plans a little, and went somewhere else after lunch?"

I put my hand over his and twined our fingers together, forcing his grip to fall away from the truck. "Of course, I don't mind." His features went both warm and cold at the same time. "What is it?"

"Badger died six months ago today," he croaked. "It just kinda hit me on the way over. I can't believe it's been half a year."

I placed my free hand over his chest, where the cross that once belonged to his friend Derrick Badger resided. "I'm so sorry, Kevin."

"I really wish you could have met him."

"Me, too. It sounds like he was a very special person." I fully believed that if our paths had ever crossed, I would have liked Badger very much. He'd made bad choices that landed him in the same cell as Kevin, but breaking the law didn't automatically make someone a bad person.

Everyone, no matter the crime, no matter the sin, was redeemable if their heart was in the right place. Kevin and Badger both had the right kind of heart, even if they hadn't always led the right kind of lives.

Kevin placed his hand on top of mine. "I've been trying to gather the guts to visit his grave all morning. It's not like I didn't know these milestones were coming, so I don't know why it's so hard."

"Grief is just one of those things you can't predict."

"It's the first time I've experienced it. I've never had anyone in my life die before. And I've never actually visited a cemetery before, either."

"And you were hoping I would go with you?"

His chest rose and fell with a heavy quiver. "Yeah. I debated even bringing this up because I wanted to just ignore it and deal so I didn't bring down the festivities. You know, the list and everything."

I cupped his face. "Kevin Ezekiel Sloan, have you forgotten what Christmas actually is? The entire point of this season is to not only celebrate the birth of Christ Himself but to live by everything He stood for, to have compassion and love for one another. I know not everyone does it that way, but as for me, it would be an honor to go visit your friend."

I could no longer hold Kevin in place as he returned my gesture, then pulled me up for a kiss that was a soft, contradicting force of its own. By the simplest of means, his emotions always became my emotions. Even after we got in the truck to leave, all I wanted to do was keep my arms wrapped around him like that forever, sustained by his warm, unremitting solace.

Forever. That word, that state of being, which Kevin was always asking me for. I knew he was teasing when he proposed, but it was obvious he meant it. He wanted to marry me, and I wanted to marry him, too, but we really were too young. I didn't have a single year of college behind me, let alone a degree or career to my name. I wasn't fully *me* yet, so there was no way I could be an *us*. We had to grow separately as much as together.

I would marry him when God told us both it was the right time. There was no doubt about that. In the meantime, life was good the way it was. Kevin wasn't going anywhere, and neither was I.

Except back to school early. My guilt picked that exact moment to remind me I hadn't yet told Kevin about the phone call about work.

Twenty minutes later, we were parked at the cemetery. I wasn't sure if he could tell how firmly he held my hand, but it didn't bother me. Praying for his peace, I stayed relaxed and gave him the only bit of comfort that I knew how to, and let him take his time.

"It sucks that God takes good people too soon. I don't get why it has to be that way."

"We can't possibly understand what *too soon* really is, or what *why* really is. All of that is up to God. That's the hardest part of faith — the trust."

"It makes so much sense to me when I'm not going through anything, then something hurts and the faith and trust becomes a struggle. I do still believe, but things hurt anyway." He rubbed the area over his heart. "I thought being a Christian was supposed to make life easier. Sunshine and rainbows even when it storms."

"A lot of times it does, but we aren't promised a pain-free life. The belief is that having faith in the storm is the way you get through it, but that doesn't mean you won't still feel the rain. I see it as more like the warm towel you come home to."

He chuckled. "That's adorable, Sarah. Wow. Faith is a warm towel." It made me happy to see his mood coming around.

"It's never easy to lose someone, Kevin. God knows that. He gave us a full spectrum of emotions because we're meant to feel them. It's okay to grieve, even six months later. Even six *decades* later. He doesn't shield us from everything, but He's there for us the whole way, every time."

When Kevin was ready, we walked over to a wrought iron bench beneath a large live oak. Badger's headstone was right in front of us, putting his name and the dates that spanned his life on display.

"When we were apart, how much did you hear about what happened in there?" came Kevin's solemn question.

"Just enough to know you were safe. I had no idea it was your cellmate until you were released and told me the whole story. I'm really glad I didn't know that part."

Without realizing it, I confirmed Kevin's point about struggling, even in faith. One could be faithful and still experience doubt, pain, fear, and worry. Those things still seeped through the minds of even the most devout Christians. That was just a fact of this fallen world. Dealing with the result of those emotions was what made the difference.

"I still can't believe how it all happened. How easily things could have been different. How it was supposed to be me that died. What makes me any better than Badger?"

"Don't say that. It was never meant to be you, or it *would* have been you. Only God chooses who to take and when. That means you're here right now for a reason."

"What reason is that?"

"The same reason as any of us. To bring people into His Kingdom."

"That's way too big of a job for me, of all people," he chided on his own behalf. "God doesn't need me on His pay roll."

"It's just the right job for you, *of all people*. You've seen the ugliest sides of life, and here you are today. You fought for yourself all your life and now you're strong enough to fight for Him."

"Still, I don't know the first thing about saving people."

"God does the saving, but we often help do the reaching. We may never see how, but He's always working through us."

I linked my arm in his and looked ahead. For a moment, we were silent while only the trees and wind did the talking.

"I still wonder who his fiancé was," he later remarked. "I should have asked her name."

"He was engaged? So young?"

"He was almost twenty-one. They were engaged before he got arrested. He said he was going to win her back when he got out."

My heart hurt for them both. "I bet she's the one who left the flowers." In a slender red vase, there were six red roses. "Six roses for six months. That's exactly the sort of detail a woman in love would think to do."

"His family was junk, so it would have to be."

"Unless they changed. Never know."

He smiled, "True."

"But my money is still on the fiancé." I smiled, too.

"You know something... when Badger told me about that Bible verse, I could never have imagined the impact it would ultimately have. That feels like such a less-than way of putting it, too."

"You see? God put Badger in your life to save you. That's not the only thing He did, but that was clearly the last bit needed to open those blind eyes. Maybe we are are only here long enough to reach at least one person."

"If that really is my purpose, I'd like to help many more than one."

"God will show you how. He loves your willing heart."

"Badger wasn't even trying to convince me. We were just having a conversation."

"Then keep that in mind the next time you talk to someone. A conversation could be all they need, too."

Kevin smiled and dislodged his arm to rub my shoulder. "Seeing this," he nodded toward the flowers, "makes me incredibly happy. I'm glad I'm not the only one who misses him."

"Me, too."

"Thanks for coming here with me, Sarah, and for all of *our* conversations over the last twelve months. You also made a huge difference in my life."

I nipped his nose with the tip of mine. "You're very welcome."

SARAH

7

2. Candy Cane Lane

Early morning on the day I drove back to Corpus, I received a phone call from my school advisor. I had applied to work in the campus daycare and had apparently been hired. Great news for my bank account, which needed a source of income to keep me less reliant on my parents while living up there. It was a good thing, I just didn't expect I would be asked to start the day after Christmas.

It almost didn't feel fair, but if they needed me to work, that meant parents needed to work. Not everyone was given the luxury of a real winter break, as the manager put it into perspective for me. It would be alright, as long as I made allowances, but I still didn't know how to tell Kevin.

The night we visited Candy Cane Lane, Tyler drove us all, with Cindie riding shotgun. The cool and crisp air had persisted, and had just enough chill to warrant a jacket. Above us and all around, thousands of Christmas lights lit up every house and yard in the neighborhood. It was a collective effort by the neighbors every year, and it never disappointed.

We parked out of the way and went on foot. Cindie and I were arm in arm, and I reflected on how easily she and I had become close since our circles had intersected. We walked at our leisure in front of the boys, who trailed behind us, chatting away about their own thing.

"Snoopy!" Cindie pointed out with an affectionate cry.

"And over there! The Grinch! He's my favorite." Charlie Brown and his four-legged buddy were fantastic, but that green-haired grump was top dog.

"That is an absolute classic. It's on my rotation of must-watch movies every year."

"Same. Kevin put *'movie night'* on our to-do list, but we've kept our choices a secret from each other. I'm excited to watch it, even though I've seen it a thousand times. He probably has, too."

"It's impossible to get tired of your favorites." She winked at me, and I knew she wasn't just taking about movies anymore. She and Tyler had been together since late spring, and they were the most perfect couple, so beautifully in sync with one another. Both were compassionate and loving and so generous. I knew right away that they were Couple Goals. I've been so happy for them.

Tyler Cortez was more than my former youth pastor. He was a friend now, closer to a brother even. And thanks to him, I'd gotten attached to Cindie, who had become a big sister to me in the process.

After she and Tyler made it official, and ever since Kevin's release, the four of us spent a lot of my time home together. Getting to know her had forged a quick path from friend to family. I had no siblings, but Cindie didn't have anyone. She had been raised by numerous foster parents and eventually aged out of state custody. She turned eighteen, moved out, and her latest foster family didn't stay in touch. Instead of making her hard and bitter, her experiences made her soft and sure. I always felt like I was in the presence of a miracle when she was around, and based on the content of her stories, it was certainly true.

"Have you and Tyler talked any more about the future?"

"I wish. He's been so cavalier. If he has any intentions at all, he's keeping them tight-lipped. I'm trying not to let it bother me because I know he has his reasons."

"I understand."

"You'd think, after the upbringing I had, that I would have perfected having patience, but that's just not me," she confided with a giggle.

"We get much better at waiting when it's God's timing we're waiting on," I said, reminding myself as much as her. "But it's not always so easy to embrace."

She squeezed my arm in the crook of her elbow, empathizing. "Amen to that. In His timing, not mine, right? If Tyler and I are meant to be, God will let me know."

I knew exactly how she felt. "And isn't that a good thing? If we had to wait around on these two, we'd be old spinsters long before we'd ever be brides."

At that, we both turned around to look at our fellas, who promptly hushed and gave us endearing looks of confusion, and our girlish giggling ensued.

"What did we miss?" Kevin's question only made us laugh more, our breaths blowing out in warm puffs.

"Nothing," Cindie sweetly promised them.

Onward we walked, enjoying the artistic expression of each home, and eventually ending up at a Santa Sleigh. Kevin and I got on the sleigh first, one of us on either side of the jolly man in red. We smiled brightly at the camera as the flash went off. Santa wished us a merry Christmas, and we collected our instant photo from his elf assistant as we got down. Mrs. Clause handed us each a small paper cup of hot chocolate and a cookie, and then Tyler and Cindie were called up for their turn.

The photographer elf smiled at Tyler and Cindie, giving them a sly wink. "Y'all are next." Glancing at Kevin to see if he'd noticed, he appeared to be none the wiser.

The rest happened in such a rush. Santa had scooted to the far end of the sleigh. Tyler extended his hand to help Cindie step aboard but stayed back.

"Are you Cindie Potter?" inquired Santa, eliciting surprise from us all.

"Yes?" Cindie answered suspiciously.

"Wonderful!" Santa reached around to the back of the sleigh and pulled on the golden drawstring of his red velvet bag. He reached inside it. "I have something in here for you." In his hand was a palm-sized present, expertly wrapped in green paper, adorned with a red ribbon, and topped with a silver bow. There was a name tag hanging from it.

Eyes wide, mouth open in shock, Cindie silently accepted the small gift. She peeled it apart with shaking fingers that had nothing to do with the cold. When the wrapping had fallen away, Cindie held up a small, gray box, completely mesmerized. She pried the top up, and I watched on, holding my breath as the scene unfolded.

While her back was turned, Cindie didn't see what else was going on. From his kneeling position on the ground, Tyler put his fist to his mouth and cleared his throat to get her attention.

Cindie whipped her head around, the ring box still open in her hands, and her jaw dropped.

"Cindie Danika Potter, *mi luna y mis estrellas*, until God brought you into my life, I didn't realize every mountain He'd placed in my path was meant to form me into the man He needed me to be, a man fit to deserve you. From the moment we met, I saw my future in you, and I knew you would help keep me striving to honor Him, and I want to be by your side doing the same for you forever. So, what do you think? Would you like to be my wife?"

Tyler had taken hold of Cindie's unsteady hands as he spoke and then slipped the ring from its box onto her finger, where her eyes were currently glued. When she looked from her glinting finger to the man in front of her, tears fell in heavy streams. "Are you sure? You want to marry *me?* Just an orphan from Kingsville?"

Tyler laughed, completely unshaken. "You're no orphan, Cindie. You're the daughter of a King. And I want to marry you more than anything else in the world," he boasted confidently.

"Good! No take-backs! Yes, a thousand times, I would love to be your wife!"

Tyler rose to his feet in a flash, collecting Cindie in his arms along the way. He pulled her clear of the sleigh and swung her around. Kevin and I were shouting and clapping, and I couldn't stop jumping up and down. Behind us, the small crowd of people that had collected were celebrating, too.

Kevin slipped his hand around mine with a firm squeeze, and even though I'd just watched two of our dearest friends get engaged, I knew I was still the luckiest one there. No mountain would hold the two of us back either, even if a small one was already trying.

KEVIN

8

3. Movie Night

SARAH'S DAD ANSWERED THE DOOR WHEN I ARRIVED.

"Hello, Kevin. How are you this afternoon?" Jonathan Stevenson asked, clutching my free hand in a stout shake.

"I'm pretty great, thanks." I held up my DVD of choice. "You going to get in on the movie marathon with us?"

"Nope, not me," he said. "I'll be tackling a bit of extra work and then spending a quiet evening with my bride."

I couldn't help but smile. "You still call her your bride? I like that."

He gave me a raised eyebrow. "Don't be liking it too much."

I shook my head. "Oh, no, sir." *If only he knew.* He might not want me thinking about his daughter in a matrimonial way, but I couldn't *wait* to make a bride out of Sarah. God willing, someday it would happen. I couldn't imagine anything or anyone on earth being able to stop me.

"Yes, well, here she is now. I will be right across the hall, where I can easily see and hear everything," he added with a

29

pointed stare. Then, after another, firmer handshake, Mr. Stevenson excused himself.

Sarah, just coming down the stairs, bid a spirited farewell to her father as she skipped the last step and bounded toward me. "Sorry, I would've answered the door, but I had to bolus for this pig-out session we're about to have."

"No worries." I held the DVD behind my back, maintaining the suspense.

"Sooo… Whatcha got there?" She tried to peek around to look, then play-pouted when I wouldn't let her.

"It's still a surprise."

"But I'm dying to know what Kevin Sloan's favorite Christmas movie of all time is."

"You'll just have to wait and see."

She gave me a playful glance as we went to the living room and got comfy. "You can go first," she announced, turning the TV on.

"Why me?"

"Because if anyone falls asleep later, I'd rather it be during my pick."

"As you wish," I touted.

After I put the DVD in, Sarah snuggled against me as I adjusted the pillows at my side. "Have I told you lately that I love your list idea? This is the single most amazing way I can imagine spending this Christmas together."

"I'm glad you like it. Hopefully I've not given us too much to do in just a few weeks, but I can tell you, it's already the best Christmas I've ever had, and we haven't even gotten there yet."

Sarah had her chin on my shoulder as I spoke. She tilted up, and I met her for a kiss. Only a brief one, much less than I craved, but I was always extra respectful in the presence of her parents.

"I love you," I whispered against her ear, grazing my lips against her cheek one last time for good measure.

"I love you, too," she whispered back, emotion lacing her words. Sarah pressed the remote buttons and started the movie, then reached for a bowl of popcorn from the coffee table. "What are you hungry for? As you can see, we have a little of everything."

There were candies, fruits, veggies, dips, popcorn, pickles — my favorite — and a variety of nuts and seeds. The delicacies were accompanied by bottles of water and juices.

"Gotta have a pickle first. Then I think I'll go with the pecans." Sarah handed everything to me as the DVD menu screen came up. I quickly put down my snacks and placed my hand across her eyes, and she laughed. "Don't look!"

The surprise didn't last much longer. The second the movie started playing, Sarah shouted, *"Home Alone*! I love this movie, too!" and pulled my hand away.

"I think literally everyone does." Settling back with my food, I took a messy bite of pickle, letting the juice fall into the cup she'd given it to me in.

"That's because it's a classic. But what makes it your *favorite?*"

I thought she might ask me that, and there wasn't a cozy answer I could give her. "You really wanna know?"

"Of course I do." She looked at me in her gentle, Sarah way, and I was convinced.

"It's dumb, but as a kid, watching it gave me a sense of power. Seeing the bad guys actually get what they deserved, and seeing a kid named Kevin dish it out... I don't know, it was insanely satis-fying." I chuckled sheepishly. "I can't tell you how many times I thought about McAllister-rigging our house to get back at Craig."

"I get that. And it's not dumb. Remember, you've fought your demons and they're not coming back. Even if they tried, you're not alone. You never were, but now you know."

Sarah's words hit all the right places, soothing my nerves and turning my thoughts back around to where they ought to be. I knew it was astounding how grateful I had become, but Sarah understood me. Sometimes, self-pity and other unwelcome traits still existed. I was made new, but not perfect. Never that.

Sarah snuggled back to my side, but rather than focusing on the movie, my mind wandered from one thing to another. What did she think about Tyler's proposal? I never had time to ask her about it. It went without saying that she was happy for them, so was I, but had it made her cogs turn at all? Was she more seriously considering a future with me after seeing the beginning of theirs? I knew *I* sure was.

But just because I wanted something, that didn't mean I would get it. That went for every Christmas that came and went without a single present, or any good cheer in sight. That even applied to a lot of other things, including school, and even a future with Sarah.

At least I didn't feel like I used to, like I could lose her at any minute. We had a really solid relationship with each other and with God, so naturally, that was an incredible help. But even that couldn't guarantee us the forever I wanted with her. Truthfully, we only had one day at a time, so I wanted each one to be the best it could be.

With a deep breath, I pushed everything in my head away and fixated only on the girl beside me and the movie in front of us. I could worry about tomorrow later.

#4 Toys for Charity

OUR TOY COLLECTION BOX AT CHURCH WAS THRIVING. LONG AFTER Pastor Brian's announcements that we were collecting, Kevin's sign was doing a great job of keeping everyone's attention. He'd painted it all by hand, in creative lettering, and dressed it up with gifts and various ornaments. Sparkly garland bordered the whole thing, topping it off just right, like the angel resting on the point of a Christmas tree.

"Your sign is just beautiful, Kevin! Jonathan, did you know Kevin could paint like that?" fussed my mom. If Kevin could have blushed, I think he would've then. He was slowly coming out of his artistic shell, but he was still very shy about his work. Compliments were still difficult for him to accept.

"Thank you, Mrs. Stevenson," he managed. He noticed the overflow, immediately redirecting the conversation. "Looks like we're gonna need a bigger box."

"I wonder if we should've put out two," I said.

"Maybe we still can. When do we take the presents to the shelter again?"

"We're meeting here this coming Friday to wrap everything, and then we'll deliver the gifts on Saturday. Oh, and I still have to get all the supplies." I'd usually be better prepared, but the weight of my secret grew heavy, clouding my mind, coming between me and my tasks.

"Should we get that done now?" Kevin looked between me and my parents. "Er, after brunch?" I corrected.

My mom smiled and waved her hand. "You guys can go. Jonathan and I can have brunch alone. We already do every Sunday you're at school, and God's work always comes first."

"Let's try out that new seafood place downtown," Dad offered.

Yuck. I made a face, not a fan of seafood at all.

Mom grimaced, for she had the same taste buds as me. "I guess I can't avoid it forever. It's a date then."

"Y'all go right ahead. Just don't forget to save room for dinner with Marie and Kevin later. You remember where their house is?"

"Sure do. We will be there at 5:30, as agreed," assured my dad, and then I saw them to the door to say goodbye.

When I turned around, I noticed Kevin talking with Pastor Brian. I hung back to not interrupt, and when they were done, he gave me a wave to join them.

"Congratulations on a successful toy campaign, Sarah. You both are doing a wonderful job. I just went by and added one more, and that might be all your box can handle."

"Thanks, Pastor. We were just talking about that."

"Go ahead and leave the sign up and we'll keep collecting. Just put another box out. We will see what more we can gather this week."

"Okay, thank you!"

"Stevenson!" I turned at the sound of my last name, only to see Tyler waving me down next.

Pastor Brian took notice and was ready to move along. "Y'all have a wonderful week. God bless."

"God bless you, too, Pastor." And off he went. He and Tyler met in the middle and said their goodbyes, and then Tyler came over. Kevin was right behind him, with the full box of presents in tow. Someone had brought him a dolly.

"What a success! Way to go, guys. What time is the wrapping party on Friday? Potluck, right?"

"It's at six, but no potluck. Erin and Glen are bringing a meal for everyone."

He slapped his hands together. "That should be delicious! You know Cindie and I will be there."

"Awesome. We're heading out to get all the supplies now, so we'll see you guys on Friday!"

"See you then."

Kevin was quiet on the way to Party City. "Everything okay?" I asked.

"Everything's fine."

"You sure? You've appeared stuck in your head ever since we left church."

"I'm fine. It's just that Pastor asked me to paint a mural in the youth room, and I don't know if I can do it," he blurted. His eyes darted between the road ahead and the rearview mirror, but he didn't look my way at all. He was so cute when he was nervous.

"Kevin! That's fantastic!"

"No, it's not. I'm going to screw it up. I've never done anything like that before. Why would he ask me?"

"Because you are an incredible painter, duh! You will not screw anything up. Do a sketch first."

"It's not that. He didn't give me a request on what to paint. That's the problem."

"You have free rein over the whole wall and that's the part you're worried about?"

"How am I supposed to come up with something to paint inside a church? I haven't even attended church for very long. What do church people want to see on the wall? I'm going to let somebody down. Somebody is going to hate it, whatever I decide."

"Don't get carried away with the negative thoughts. None of that is true. You could always ask Pastor for suggestions or advice. I'm sure he would steer you right. But also pray on it. You can't go wrong. I believe in you."

He sighed and let his head fall back against the headrest as we waited at a red light.

"You could even ask your mom for her input. She's still going to her church on the island, right?"

"Yeah."

"Then she might have some great ideas for you about what 'church people' might like."

"Why can't you tell me? Aren't you 'church people'?"

"I don't have a creative bone in my body! You don't want my advice. Just remember, Pastor Brian asked you for a reason. He believes in you, too. You're talented, Kevin. Insanely so. God gave you that gift, and He will tell you how to use it, one way or another. Just let Him speak."

Kevin reached over and wound our fingers together, then lifted them and placed a kiss on my knuckles. "Thank you. I'll try."

KEVIN

10

"Remind me again. Who all is coming tonight?" Sarah's auburn waves were falling out of the knot atop her head as we pushed and pulled tables, arranging them for the wrap party.

"Besides Glen and Erin, there will be Tyler, Cindie, Sammy, Birdie, and Jared, I believe."

"No Jenna?"

"She isn't feeling well."

"Well, that can't be helped. Poor thing."

"We can add her to the prayer list."

"Good idea." Sarah shuffled another chair, then shook out a fresh tablecloth before taping it down around the edges. "Hey, so, are you going to be okay with Jared?"

"Sure. He doesn't really bother me anymore. Much." I was changed, but not perfect, I reminded myself again.

"Good, I'm glad. We've all come a long way."

"Yeah, too much has happened for us to continue fighting. It doesn't make any sense anymore. Everyone has moved on."

"Exactly," she said, taking a step back and resting her hands on her hips. Her eyes wandered to the table near the window, where all the supplies were waiting. Her approval and excitement were palpable. "I think we're ready to roll."

The side door swung open and Tyler held it, stepping out of the way. "Hello, hello!" Cindie carried a large round pie dish while Tyler held the door open for her.

"Hey, guys! You're early."

"Tyler convinced me to make one of my Dutch apple pies, so I wanted to get it here to the kitchen as soon as possible to keep it warm."

"Ooh, Cindie. That is my favorite pie!" Sarah pranced over to inspect the dish. She leaned down with a deep inhale and clapped. "You made this from scratch? You are my new favorite person."

"Hey." I splayed my arms in a *what about me* type of way.

Sarah turned to me, eyes sympathetic. "But she has pie."

"Fine, fine. I see how it is. Just don't come crawling back to me when you're down to crumbs and remember how amazing I am."

"I won't because Cindie can bake a whole lot better than we can. I will always have the best deserts to keep me happy!"

Much laughter later, when the entire party was assembled, we opened with a fellowship prayer and then blessed the meal. Once everyone's plates were cleared, we got right down to business.

The groups naturally separated themselves by gender, and I found myself at a table with Tyler, Jared, and Glen. I knew little about Erin's husband, but Glen seemed like a cool guy. And he sure knew how to wrap!

"How did you learn to do that?" I couldn't help but wonder as my eyes jumped from my current atrocity to the masterpiece in front of him.

He looked at me very matter-of-fact. "Have you ever had children?"

I chuckled. "No, sir."

"Then you don't have any grandchildren." Glen's quirkiness didn't always make sense, but it was enjoyable.

"Definitely not."

"Well, that's how. After all the Christmases I've spent playing Santa, I've got the wrapping thing down to a science."

"That's the trick then, huh? It'll be a while before either of us reach your level of mastery, Glen," Tyler laughed. His pile of gifts wasn't a whole lot better looking than mine. They would stay put together, but they wouldn't win any awards for prettiness.

"You both have plenty of time. But believe me, you will learn." Glen grabbed a blue bow from the heap of decorations and peeled the backing off. With a final *'voila!'* he slapped it on top of his latest present.

Tyler, Jared, and I all looked at one other.

I shook my head in amazement. "At least I know how to draw," I said, tooting my poor sad horn.

"Yeah, I heard something about that!" Tyler exclaimed. "Pastor Brian tells me you've agreed to concoct something for our empty youth room."

Heat burned my face, and I resisted my typical urge to sink into my chair and fade away. I didn't look up from my wrapping paper, but I could feel all the excited eyes looking my way. Even the girls behind us were sneaking glances. I could feel it all.

My suspicions were confirmed when I heard Sarah brightly command the subject at her table, bringing up the disastrous cookies we made the other day.

I smiled to myself and then dealt with the topic of discussion in front of me. "He has asked me to paint a mural for the youth room, yes. But I haven't been able to come up with anything yet."

"Did he give you any sort of parameters for it?"

"Just that he hopes it fills that entire wall, and that it should be something that represents the spirit of the church. Like I'm the best guy to decide something like that, of all people."

"Which wall, exactly?"

"The one on the right, just as you enter."

"That's a big wall," Tyler agreed. "What an amazing opportunity."

I couldn't argue with that.

"You shouldn't feel like the wrong guy for the job. Pastor Brian is a smart man. He has been at this nearly his entire life. When I discussed changing up the youth room, he knew right away those changes should include your art. If he's chosen you to embellish the church with your creativity, then his confidence is well-placed."

"Are you on a deadline?" Jared asked, sitting back in his chair and taking a break from his task.

"No."

"So, you can paint anything you want, and you have no deadline to get it done?"

Sarah had basically said the same thing. "Yeah…"

"Then what are you worried about?" Jared's question wasn't rude or unwarranted, but I didn't get how to explain it to him. He didn't know me like that.

But I did know I was overreacting. I had Sarah, I had Jesus, I had my mom, and I had our wonderful friends. We all had more than enough. I didn't need to let worry consume me at a time like this, try though it may.

"You'll figure it out, Kev." Jared and I were civil, but it was still a little weird when he addressed me.

"Thanks, man. I'm sure you're right." Less sure than I wanted to be, but I had to get there. What choice did I have?

There was only one way to find out. I decided right then that as soon as I got home, I would begin drafting out some ideas. In the meantime, I had to think about what the spirit of the church was. As I looked around the room at everyone there that evening, I thought it must look something like that. People spending their time sowing seeds they wouldn't reap any benefits from. Selflessness must have something important to do with it, or it wouldn't feel so right.

11

#5 Fire & Hot Chocolate

My legs were crossed tightly under me, covered by my favorite throw, courtesy of my dad's recliner, and I had Kevin's favorite black sweatshirt on, the hood pulled over my head and the strings drawn down. I sighed into the night, luxuriating in the warmth that surrounded me.

I could be outside like this every single day, if only the Texas weather was this amiable all the time. Sometimes I questioned if I was living in the wrong state, but I know I could never leave my home state.

"This is the best."

"Yes, it is." Kevin looked around, his chest puffing up with silent pride as he took in my compliment.

Over the past several months, Kevin had transformed his backyard into a little oasis. The grass no longer grew wild. Now it was beautifully trimmed and watered, and miraculously ant-free. Not even my mom could figure that one out, and she took meticulous care of our own.

The fruit trees he'd planted were rooting strong, as well as the berry bushes that now lined his fence line. Two crepe myrtles waved, bold and secure, from where he'd torn out thorny huisache trees. It had become a beautiful wonder, and we loved spending quiet moments out there together.

The fire pit he dug out and lined with scalloped cinder blocks was ablaze with flickering life. The breeze swirled just enough to make it dance, without the risk of sending it flying or snuffing it out. In my hands, my hot chocolate provided a distinctive delight with each inhalation.

Between us, on a TV tray doubling as a patio table, a small Bluetooth speaker played a variety of hymnals and songs of the season. I was humming along, bouncing my foot, and sipping my drink as I took refuge in the moment.

"So, this is number five on our list. That means we're halfway through it. Are you enjoying our little adventure so far?" Kevin watched the firelight and sipped his hot chocolate.

"Very much! I am continually impressed by how sweet you are."

"I wonder if we're going through them too fast. Maybe we should draw them out more or something."

A slight tremor shook me, having nothing whatsoever to do with the cold. "If we do that, we might not get to finish before Christmas." I had been close to slipping up and reminding him I had to go back to school after Christmas Day, rather than the week after, but I remembered I still hadn't mustered the guts to tell him yet.

Concern turned into guilt more and more with each day that passed, but I didn't know how to stop my bad news from robbing us of the good time we were having.

Kevin noticed the way my eyes pooled in the corners. "Hey, you okay?"

Straightening my back, I played it off. "I'm fine, just catching a lot of the smoke." I waved as though annoyed with it, feeling the liability trickle up my spine.

I sipped my chocolate and, from the corner of my eye, watched Kevin observe the smoke from the fire. The wind was blowing it in the opposite direction, but for whatever reason, he chose not to press me on it.

Maybe he was dealing with something of his own and didn't want to draw attention to anything serious. He did seem to not be quite himself tonight. During a time like this when we would normally chat and laugh together, he was really quiet. If *I* was quiet and there was a reason for it, then it only made sense that his quiet would mean something, too.

That would have to be a mystery solved on another day. I didn't want to push him when I knew I didn't want him to pull.

Kevin broke this round of silence. "You want any more marshmallows?"

"No, thank you. I actually don't even like them," I admitted, swirling them around the inside edge of my mug.

"Why did you ask for them then?"

"Just to have the full experience." I smiled. "I can tolerate a few squishy white bits in exchange for a picture perfect hot chocolate."

"In that case..." Kevin reached over and grabbed the bag of marshmallows. Tearing the hole in the corner even bigger, he tipped it over and dumped the rest of them into his mug. It didn't take long for it to fill, and then little white puffs were spilling out all over the place.

"What are you doing!?" I laughed, trying to catch them as they ran over.

"Having a picture perfect hot chocolate experience!" He held out his mug. "Cheers!"

Taking a handful of his overflow off the top, I redistributed them to my own. "Cheers!"

We drank, and then our familiar mirth and conversation returned. He moved the table to the other side of his chair and moved mine closer, so we were shoulder to shoulder. I draped my blanket over him, tucking us in. We remained that way until the fire died out. It was long enough for me to forget, at least for the moment, what would be my too-soon departure.

KEVIN

12

THE TIME FINALLY CAME FOR ME TO PAINT THE MURAL AT CHURCH. Tyler went out to meet me there right at 7 A.M that morning. I backed my truck into the closest parking spot I could, so my supplies and I had less distance to travel.

My arsenal included everything from brushes to palettes to paints and everything in between. I thought about trying a stencil and transfer paper for a project this big, but I wasn't familiar enough with the process to ensure justice was done. All I had was a basic sketch, and that was the best I could do.

Still baffled, I couldn't understand why Tyler and Pastor Brian trusted me with this task. I didn't feel qualified, and not in the sense of technical skill. I knew I could paint this wall, and it wouldn't look half bad. But how did I know if I was painting the right thing?

Why couldn't they have given me more direction? Presumably, they thought they were doing me a favor, giving me so much creative control, but the freedom was nearly debilitating.

God, what do I paint? Please, guide my hands and keep my mind on You. Don't let me let these people down.

Even after all my prayers, I still had no idea what would be going up there, but it was time to get started.

Sarah was sleeping in this morning. I insisted, after our late night last night. Plus, I thought I would work better without an audience. I'd gotten comfortable with her being around me while I drew, but this was different. Tyler was staying there, but he was working on lesson plans and correspondence, so he would not be watching me.

I needed this to be between me and God. That was the only way I could see myself pulling it off. The right idea *had* to come to me.

Just as I set down my last tote full of stuff, Tyler came around with a ladder. "This is for you, *mi amigo.*" He opened it up, and it was about half my size. It was just tall enough to get me to where I'd need to reach with no need for a spotter.

I stood there awkwardly. "Perfect. Thank you."

"You look a little frazzled. You okay?"

"Yeah, I'm fine."

"You sure?"

"I'm a little nervous, but I will manage."

"I know that's true. But just the same, would you care for me to pray with you before we get to work?"

"Sure. That would be fine." I could use all the help I could get, and I promptly closed my eyes.

Tyler stepped closer and reached his right arm out to my shoulder. His left hand rested on the crown of my head. He eased into the act with such care and gentleness. No sooner had his mouth opened, than I could *feel* Tyler's prayer.

"Lord Jesus, I thank You every day for bringing this sheep into Your fold, and pray Your many blessings over all facets of Kevin's life. This morning I also pray anointing over his painting. Speak

Your will for his brush, and reach out your Mighty hand for every stroke. Lift him up with Your Spirit as only You can. I pray for You to make a move here for Kevin, Lord, so he has the confidence to glorify You to the highest. In Your beautiful name, Jesus, AMEN."

"Amen. Thank you, Jesus."

Soon enough, I felt a rush of peace, a gentle wave of assuredness that I *was* the right person for this job. I had been asked on behalf of the church, but I wanted to make God proud above all others. I realized it wasn't Pastor Brian or even Tyler who had truly entrusted me with this task. It was God Himself.

As he took a step back, Tyler smiled. "I have a feeling about this one, Kev. You've got this. I'll text you later to check in, but give me a holler if you need anything."

"Will do. Thanks, Tyler."

When I was left alone, I rolled my shoulders and grabbed my first brush. The wall had been primed the day before, so I was ready to rock. With my wide set brush, I started on the background.

Despite having brought a sketch with me, the scene that unfolded in my head was new and amazing, and as it took hold in my heart, I knew it was meant to be.

With every dip in the paints and each stroke of the brushes, I watched the big picture come to life. Most people would've taken a break, would've needed one, but I worked as though time stood still. I knew nothing else but the imagery in front of me.

I brought back an old friend, an American bald eagle, wings spread proud and wide across the whole top of the wall. Edge to edge, it reached. The eyes shone a glimmering gold and white. From the middle of it expanded a large circular tomb, which glowed radiant with streams of light. And within that glowing light was the faintest silhouette of Jesus following the resurrection.

He is risen. It wasn't just a fun term thrown around during Easter to combat the worldly bunnies and candy; it was a universal truth all the time.

All along the bottom, spanning out on both sides beneath the wingspan, were unspecific figures. Representations of all the people of the earth — past, present, and future. The light engulfed them, just like it would everyone someday.

I painted all day and came back the following morning. It was past noon on the second day before I finished. Once I had cleaned up, I made my way to Tyler's office where he was again patiently waiting for me to paint in peace. He had fallen asleep in his chair.

Though I gingerly tapped on the door, he startled awake. "Kevin! Oh wow, I fell asleep? I am so sorry. Is everything okay?"

"It's just fine. I'm done with the mural."

"Done? Like completely?" He checked his watch, and in disbelief, compared it to his phone. "I can't believe I slept all this time. I must've really needed that. But wait, are you really done already?"

"Yep. Still have to get my stuff back in the truck, but the wall is d-o-n-e — *done.*"

"That's excellent! Let me see this wall of yours." He got up and followed me through the office into the youth room. He'd promised not to peek when I left the night before, so he was seeing it now for the first time. When he looked, I didn't feel too nervous to watch his face. I knew the mural was just right.

"*Aye,* wow, Kevin... This is more beautiful than I imagined it would be. No wonder you didn't let me see it earlier. Do you know how well you've done? This is truly something."

"I have an idea." I smiled. "It came to me right on time and felt too right for me to doubt it."

"I'm so glad to hear that. It's such a joyous day when we can set ourselves aside and let Him do the heavy lifting. This image right here is an incredible example."

"For sure. There's no way I could have come up with this whole thing on my own. I did find it funny, though. I used to draw this eagle in my sketchbooks all the time, especially in class. Sarah called me out on it once," I laughed. "All that time, God was chasing after me in a language He thought I might understand, but I didn't then. I do now, and it's crazy what I can look back on and see."

Tyler nodded, a bright smile on his face. "Yes. Yes. That's how He does things. Now you have the eyes to see and the ears to hear, Kevin. Just don't close them."

"It helps that you know how to deliver an amazing prayer." Had to hand it to him. I might not have been in a quiet enough place to let God's image come through the noise without Tyler's help. I'd been trying.

Yesterday morning, I had come with my own agenda in mind, sketch in hand, and even though I thought it would do, He turned my heart from my idea and instructed me to create something else.

I had been so worried for nothing, when all I had to do was stand present in faith and let Him do the rest.

Oh, how much He speaks when we listen.

Tyler nudged me on the shoulder with his fist. "Thanks, Kev. But it's all Him," he emphasized by looking skyward. "Now, what do you say we get this all loaded up, and I treat you to some tacos? It's the least I can do since my room is now the coolest in the entire building."

My stomach rumbled in agreement, finally speaking up for its due. "That sounds great." I wasn't expected to meet up with Sarah for another couple of hours, anyway. We had another item to check off the list, and we wouldn't grab food until after. "Oh, hey. Are you and Cindie going to Callie's play tonight?"

"I really wish we were, but we couldn't get out of our plans. I hadn't heard about it until a couple of days ago."

"I think they're streaming it as well, so you could go back and watch it later."

"Oh, good to know! We'll do that. Thank you."

We collected all my supplies and loaded them into the back of my truck. Before we left, I took one last glance at the mural and snapped a picture. Not to send it to anyone, I just wanted it for myself. I was excited for Sarah to see it in person come Sunday morning, and I would invite my mom to our church this weekend, too. She will definitely want to see it in person.

As I walked out and followed Tyler into town, I was still overcome with the greatest sense of peace. It was unlike anything I had felt in a good while. How grateful was I that somebody like me, so busted up and beyond saving as I assumed I was, had become a vessel for the Almighty God? If He had given me this talent, the least I could do was use it for His purpose, as Sarah was saying.

The more I embraced that thought, I found that more ideas took form in my head. I knew I wanted to keep painting, but I needed to only worry about one thing at a time. The mural was done, so for now, I had done enough.

Up next was number six on the list. Taking Sarah to see a Christmas play.

SARAH

13

#6 Christmas Play

Even though we weren't supposed to have one, Callie Olivarez was my favorite student from Children's Church. Anytime I went in as a helper, she clung to me like glue. I had no want of a little sister when she was around to fill the position so well. She simply adored me and the feeling was more than mutual.

Last Sunday, she invited Kevin and me to watch her perform in her school's Christmas play. Originally, Kevin had wanted to take me to see *The Nutcracker* in San Antonio, but when I told him about sweet Callie's invitation, we agreed to make her play our number six instead. That was probably the best compromise we'd ever made.

Callie's third-grade performance of *A Christmas Carol* was at her school on the west side of town. Kevin informed me it was the same one he had attended, and he recalled being forced to take part in a play or two in his day.

On the drive over, I turned to him. "So, what was little Kevin like when you were in those plays? How old were you?"

I could tell he was simply thrilled by the questioning. Possibly, he regretted his decision to divulge that information earlier, but the idea was just too cute not to have all the details.

"First one, I was around Callie's age. I avoided any others until spring of sixth grade."

"Didn't you have any fun at all? What plays were they?"

"The first one was a Christmas one just like this. It was probably even the same play, but I honestly can't remember. I hated it so much. I begged not to participate."

"How come?"

"Are you kidding? Dressing up and getting on stage in front of tons of people? I was so embarrassed."

Aw. Poor little Kevin. "I bet it was beyond adorable. What about the sixth grade one?"

"That one, I did willingly, because rehearsal kept me away from home for longer, and — yeah."

That sounded interesting. "What does *'and yeah'* mean?"

"Nothing, really."

"You can't do that! I want to know."

"No, you don't."

"Yes, I do. Come on, out with it."

He sighed. "I auditioned because my crush was in it. She was all about drama, the theatrical kind, and — *yeah*."

"Aww," I cooed, imagining a shy, young Kevin stepping out like that, hoping his crush would notice him. "That's so sweet."

"Seriously? I thought it would bother you."

"Kevin, you were what? Twelve? That's hardly impeding on my territory."

He chuckled, his crooked smile taking hold. "I guess you're right."

"Plus, that's precious. What a sweet guy you are. I'm so glad you're mine." I reached over and pinched his cheek.

"Tell me, Sarah. Do you have any old crushes I need to worry about?"

"Well, that depends on what Brandon McKinney is doing these days, but boy oh boy, back in kindergarten, I was smitten. He always shared his bubblegum and crayons with me.

"Those are some pretty high standards."

"I know."

Kevin's chest quickly deflated. "I don't think there's any point in trying. We should just look him up so I can hand you over."

"Sounds like it's for the best. This has been nice while it lasted, but I guess you can't stop true love."

"I guess so, because nobody's touching my crayons."

KEVIN'S GAZE turned to the school after helping me down from the truck. "Jeez, this place hasn't changed at all."

"Get your fill because apparently they're tearing it down."

"What?"

"Yep. Callie told me they're going to be in portables for a few months at the start of next year because of the new construction."

"That... kinda sucks. Weird."

"What's weird?"

"I wouldn't have thought I would care about something like that, but there goes a constant stream of memories. Typically a school stays long after you leave it, but there's something oddly comforting about it still being there. It's like part of you remains, and your memories can never go away." Kevin peered thoughtfully across the parking lot to the large building. "Now, it feels like something inside me will be demolished with it."

"Wow. You couldn't have put that any better. You're so right. If they ever try to tear down Corpus Christi High School, we must protest." The early years for me were one thing, but high school was where I met Kevin. Those memories were never allowed to leave the area, even if we did.

I was aware that wasn't something anyone could really help, but still.

When we were seated inside, Kevin was fascinated by his recollection of the auditorium seats. "It is really like time has been frozen for the last decade. These are the literal same seats. The smell of this room is exactly the same, even though countless things and people come and go from it day in and day out."

"I'll bet."

He ran his hands over the armrests thoughtfully. "Too bad I don't have video of those plays. Then you could see it, too."

"I would have loved to see them. But it's pretty cool to be here with you, just the same." He rubbed his thumb over mine.

"Have you seen Callie yet?" he asked, glancing around.

Not that we should have been able to, but we'd already seen a dozen or more children popping out of the curtain to check on the audience. As people poured in, more peeking faces appeared and then disappeared when the drama teacher reeled them back in like slippery fish in a pond.

"No, not yet. But I'm sure it won't be long."

As though she had been summoned, I heard Callie's tiny but mighty voice behind me. We both turned, and she came trotting down the aisle, heading right toward us in the front row.

I stood up and caught her as she jumped.

"Hey, Sarah!"

"Hey, Callie! Are you feeling ready for your theater debut?" I asked, lowering her to her feet. Kevin was still seated beside me, waiting.

"I'm so excited but so scared. What if I trip or forget my lines?"

"I understand your worries. I would be concerned, too." Tapping my finger on my chin, I had an idea. "Let's see... Do you have your shoelaces tightly knotted?"

She looked down, holding up one foot, then the other for my inspection.

"Both look perfect. No tripping hazard then. And what about your lines? Do you have many?"

She nodded.

"Would you recite your favorite one for me really quick? Just as a special sneak peek?"

Her dimples took over her face as her smile widened, and she recited her line. It was from the second half of the second act, just before the climax.

"That was beautiful, Callie! You're a natural! Now, what is your least favorite line?"

I watched as she intently recited what she deemed boring, and I would've thought was the most exciting part of the whole play. I was immensely intrigued by how this entire production was going to go.

"Callie, you did fantastic! You have obviously studied very hard on your lines, so there's no reason to think you'll forget any. Right?"

"Yeah! Right!"

"But just in case you're still feeling nervous on stage, I want you to remember something…" Putting my hand down against my side and wiggling my fingers at him, I gave Kevin the signal.

He stood, stepping around me and holding up the bouquet of pink roses we picked up on the way over. Callie's eyes went like saucers.

"Are those for me!?"

"Yes, ma'am, they are," Kevin answered. "But how about I hold on to them during the show? That way, if you get nervous, you can look over at us and see them, and remember you have something to look forward to afterward. You just gotta get through this show first."

I grabbed her little hand. "No matter how you do tonight, you're already a star. And stars get flowers after performances."

"Those are so pretty! They're like pink princess flowers! Like the ones my grandma grows out on the ranch. She would really like those."

"They are all yours!" I smiled.

She grinned so big and jumped up and down. "Thank you, thank you, thank you!" Then she leaped for me and I caught her again. "Could I take one out of the bunch and give it to someone?"

"Of course you can. They're yours, and sharing is caring."

"Thanks," she said, her face pooling with color.

Mrs. Wood stuck her head out from behind the curtain, and her scowl turned into frantic relief when she found the object of her search. "Callie Olivarez, you wily coyote! You need to get up here right now!"

She jumped. "Ah! I'm coming!" Turning to us, "I'll be back for those roses!" she promised, and then ran up the side stage stairs, waving as she retreated behind the curtain.

Kevin and I sat back in our seats and watched how much

more full the auditorium had become. In a matter of minutes, the lights were dimmed and the steady stream of talking faded. All that remained was the soft shuffling of last-minute arrivals and the reprimanding hushing coming from backstage.

The spotlight turned on and Mrs. Wood emerged from the center divide in the curtain, to which we all applauded. She introduced the show and sang praises for the children's hard work, instructing us all to enjoy. I shimmied to a comfortable position in my seat and knew very well that I would.

SARAH

14

Callie made many glances at the flowers in Kevin's lap, both discreetly and not so much so. She didn't forget any lines and was the cutest darn Ghost of Christmas Past that ever existed.

When the bowing had concluded and the lights and curtains were raised for the last time, Callie was the first one to bound off the stage. Her makeup was smudged, and she hadn't gone back to change out of her costume. She wanted her flowers, and Kevin was happy to oblige.

"Here you are, miss. You've really earned them. That was a wonderful performance."

"Thank you! I love them so much! Don't tell my mommy, but they're even prettier than the ones she got me."

We were still giggling when she was once again ushered away, beckoned backstage to change. Kevin and I spoke with Callie's parents for a few minutes and congratulated them on having such a superstar for a daughter as we all waited for her to return. We couldn't possibly leave without a proper goodbye. She'd never forgive us.

Soon, she came back and handed her pink bouquet to her mom.

Then, with one hand behind her back, she approached us. Specifically, Kevin. Barely looking up from her toes, Callie brought her hands around and then held one of her pink roses out to him. "Here."

"For me? Are you sure?" She nodded. "Wow, thank you so much, little lady." Kevin reached his free arm out and hugged her shoulder. In return, Callie squeezed his torso tightly with both arms. Then, quickly breaking away, she did the same to me.

Then she put her hands on my shoulders to bring down my ear. "I promise I'm not trying to steal him."

Softly, I giggled and whispered back, "That's good news, because I don't think I could compete with an actress."

We all said goodnight and went our separate ways. Back in the truck, Kevin and I were discussing the play.

"That was so cute. They all did so good." Kevin's opinion said it all.

"They sure did. But who knew I'd end up with such a fierce adversary of my own?"

Kevin laughed. "It's too bad I don't have a little brother."

Possessively taking hold of his arm, I agreed. "Too bad is right because I'm not giving you up. You'll just have to start sharing those crayons, buddy."

"I guess I will."

WE WERE STANDING outside my house after the play when the sky did something incredible.

Kevin's eyes were fixated skyward. "Do you see that?"

"Is it really what I think it is?"

Mesmerized by the tiny white specks as they floated down, I held my arm out to catch one. Several of them collected and pooled to create tiny droplets of water as they hit the warmth of my hand. "It's snowing!?"

"It's snowing," he parroted my surprise. "I didn't know it was cold enough for this. Ever."

I cupped my hands, trying to see if I could get one to last for longer than two seconds, but each one melted faster than the last.

"I heard something about it on the radio on the drive down here. They were saying it was possible but unlikely. I had completely forgotten. I can't believe it. Do you remember seeing the snow when it happened forever ago?"

"Yep. That was the one and only time, and it didn't stick at all. It just came down and hit and then was gone."

"That's how I remember it, too. Very disappointing for something so exciting. I hope it stays around long enough to build a snowman this time."

"I'd call that possible but unlikely, Sloan, but if it does, you have to come over right away. You're the only one I want to build a snowman with."

"I'll plan to be here first thing in the morning, just in case."

We said our own goodbyes and, long after Kevin's truck had disappeared from the neighborhood, I stood outside enjoying the snow. Out there by myself, I could *hear* it falling. The flakes were big and steady and, after twenty minutes, I could see a bit of accumulation on the ground. I didn't want to get my hopes up, this was the south after all, but I would dig out an old scarf just in case the world was white when I woke up tomorrow.

In the morning, there was a modest blanket of remaining snow cover. It wasn't very thick and it wouldn't last for long, but

Kevin was on my doorstep bright and early to enjoy it with me, just as he'd said.

My scarf was wound comfortably around my neck, and I was warm inside my heavy coat. A handful of neighborhood kids had the same idea and were already stomping green footprints into the snow and throwing snowballs all around. That looked like it could be fun, too. Maybe Kevin and I would get in on that.

"What should we do first?" I questioned, stepping out.

Kevin smirked, pulled aside the heavy flaps of his jacket, and into the pocket of his hoodie beneath it. He produced a long, fat carrot with one hand, and a handful of polished stones with the other. "I have the perfect plan. Do you have an extra scarf we could use?"

KEVIN

15

#7 Tree Lighting Ceremony

Downtown was packed, and I was glad we'd gone early. We would have a little ways to walk since we parked at my mom's, but that would be easier than fighting everyone near the tree trying to leave all at the same time.

Mom decided not to go with us, even though Sarah and I both thought she should.

"That's one of the biggest perks of this view. I can see everything from the comfort of my own front porch."

Undoubtedly, her view was incredible. It struck me all over again every time I went to visit. But seeing it from afar wasn't the same as going and standing around it with the crowd.

"Fair enough, but it would still be fun."

"I'm over that kind of fun. I like my space, and not sharing it with hundreds of other people. You guys will have plenty of fun without me."

Sarah let out a little laugh. "We can come back here and have a cup of coffee or something before we go home if you'd like?"

"Great idea, Sarah. What do you think, Mom?"

"Sure, honey, if y'all want. I'll be here."

I nodded, satisfied. "We'll see you later tonight then."

A little while later, we were gathered together with those hundreds of other people, all shoulder to shoulder, waiting for the tree to be lit. Some were dancing while music spilled out from multiple speakers.

Sarah turned to me. "I'm still sad the snow is gone."

"Me too."

"Frosty has no form left, poor thing. He's barely hanging in there."

"We'll see him again someday, or so I hear."

She chuckled. There were seven minutes left on the clock when her phone rang.

"Hey, Mom," Sarah answered.

"Hey, baby. How's the tree?" Her voice was as clear as a bell despite all the surrounding noise.

"It's great. Huge turnout. Only six minutes to go."

"If you have time afterward, can you ask Marie if she needs us to bring anything for dinner tomorrow?"

"Sure, I can do that. We're going back over there tonight to hang out for a bit before I come home."

"Oh, good. You should spend as much time with her and Kevin as you can. Your dad and I were actually talking about having everyone over for lunch before you go back to school on Thursday. Thought that might be nice."

My mind balked. "What did she say?" Thursday was the day after Christmas. There's no way I heard that right. But the anxious way Sarah looked at me, phone still pressed against her ear, I knew it had to be true.

I held her gaze until she turned away.

"Yeah, Mom. We'll see. I gotta go now."

There were four minutes left on the clock, but the ceremony held no more appeal. They could shoot the tree up into outer space for all I cared. I was ready to be anywhere else, away from everyone else.

"Okay, honey. See you later. Have a good time."

"Thanks, Mom. Bye."

Sarah stuffed her phone into the pocket of her jacket and moved in front of me. She squared her jaw and took a deep breath. "I didn't know how to tell you." Her tone was undeniably apologetic. Any other time and it would have crumbled me.

"Not like this," I stated firmly, my disappointment seeping out angrily.

"I'm so sorry. I just wanted to avoid this exact thing. We've been having an amazing time."

"And we wouldn't have if you'd told me the truth from the beginning? How long have you known about this?"

"Since the day I came home. I got the phone call in the car. I have to start work right away after Christmas."

I didn't respond. Wouldn't even look at her, but from the corner of my eye, I could see her repentant gaze turn glossy. Was she upset because she got caught or because I was mad about it?

Both? Neither?

The final countdown rang out around us.

"TEN. NINE. EIGHT. SEVEN. SIX. FIVE. FOUR. THREE. TWO. ONE."

Cheering and clapping ensued as the thousands of lights and ornaments on the giant tree lit up with brilliant splendor. The speakers played "Hark the Herald Angels Sing." All around us, people were hugging, kissing, clapping, and there *we* were at the start of a fight. Our first in so long, I couldn't remember the last one. I wanted to be joyful like everyone else, but my heart felt twisted.

Sarah was really leaving the day after Christmas? But she practically just got here. That hurt like I didn't expect, but it was worse that she hadn't told me about it up front. I couldn't be mad at her for getting a job, but at the moment, because of how it had played out, I was unable to be happy for her, either.

The more in my head I stayed, the angrier I became, and the more ridiculous I felt. We shouldn't be turning on each other at a time like this. I had so little to give her as it was. My reaction just felt like a strike against me, but I was only human, and Sarah had kept something important from me. Was there ever a chance that was going to go well?

Sarah and I watched the rest of the ceremony in silent contradiction to those around us. When it ended, we walked back to my mom's in continued silence. Was I overreacting? Probably, but I couldn't help myself.

As we approached my mom's building, Sarah headed toward the parking lot rather than the elevator.

"Where are you going? What happened to going up and seeing my mom first?"

She stopped, turning. "Aren't you taking me home?"

"Kevin, I couldn't fake a smile right now if I tried. I can't face her while we're like this. You can barely stand to look at me as it is. It's probably best if I just go home."

No, we can't waste time. I didn't know how little we had.

But my foolish pride wouldn't let me tell her that. My true feelings were kept buried stubbornly beneath it.

"Fine. Yeah, let's call it a night." Forging past her, I went to the lot.

"I don't want you to be mad at me, Kevin."

"We don't always get what we want, do we?"

"Come on…" Sarah pleaded with me, one hand on the door handle. "We can start fresh tomorrow, can't we? I will meet you back here and we'll have breakfast with your mom to make up for tonight."

"We already have plans tomorrow, remember?"

She thought for a moment. "Oh, yeah. Well, we could do both, if you want. I'm sure we can fit it in early enough."

My shoulders quickly rose and fell. Defeat could have me. I didn't want to deal with this anymore tonight. She couldn't make up for it by making deals with me, I just had to cool off. "It's fine. We will have our hands full with the dinner anyway." I opened my door. "Let's just go." Sarah remained beside the truck, speechless, as I got in.

Her sadness made me feel bad, but wouldn't letting her off the hook this quickly betray my own hurt feelings? Eventually we would have to talk about it, but not yet. I wasn't able to brush it off and pretend it was okay any more than I wanted to waste the rest of her time at home fighting. We would get past it, but first, I needed a breather.

SARAH

16

"I'M SO SORRY, HONEY. I DID NOT KNOW YOU HADN'T TOLD HIM, OR that he could hear me. Why exactly had you not told Kevin?" My mom adjusted in her seat as we ate breakfast together alone. Dad was at the office early, making up some hours so he could be off tonight. He was always busy during the holiday season.

"I know. Not telling him was stupid, but I got in my head. Sharing the news of my new job meant ruining the time we had left together, and I didn't want to spoil his Christmas. It's our first one together. He wanted it to be extra special for me. He made me this amazing list of beautiful things to do and everything. My news would have only crushed him sooner."

"Oh, honey, not everything is so extreme. You didn't ruin anything. Honesty goes a lot further up front than an apology later, but I'm certain he will forgive you. You did wrong, but you meant well."

"You should've seen his face last night." I groaned, throwing my head down into my folded arms.

"I imagine he was pretty upset, sure. But to say you ruined anything is just ridiculous. It will not change a thing."

"Well, it's already 11 A.M., and he still hasn't texted me."

Mom laughed. "So? Do you guys text each other every minute of the day?"

"No, but he always texts me good morning. It's a thing." I fidgeted with my remaining breakfast.

"What if he's not awake yet?"

My forehead creased. "He's always up earlier than this, but obviously it is a possibility." How did I not think of that on my own?

"Or he could just be busy, too. He is human, you know. There are a million possible reasons why he hasn't texted you yet, and not even a fraction of them are as bad as you imagine." She reached over and patted my hand. "I understand how you're feeling, Sarah, but I promise you have done no irreparable damage. Just give him a bit and when he's ready, make your apology. Explain. And then move right along. Be done with it and enjoy. Reality is, you are leaving early whether anyone likes it or not, so don't spend your time fighting over the details."

As usual, Mom was right, and I was feeling ridiculous. That didn't stop me from watching the clock tick painfully by, until at last, my phone vibrated. I breathed easily again when I saw it was Kevin.

"By the way," Mom said, standing up and taking away my neglected plate. "Good job keeping up with your insulin. Your numbers have been looking great. I know it's not always easy to behave during these months when extra sweets and heavy eating are the norm."

"Thanks, Mom. I've been doing my best."

"That's all we can ever do." She watched the direction of my eyes and my antsy demeanor and put two and two together. "Alright, alright. Go answer your phone."

KEVIN

Good morning

SARAH

Good morning 😊 I'm glad to hear from you.

KEVIN

I know I'm late to text, sorry. My mom and I were
out early shopping for dinner stuff

SARAH

Oh yeah, of course.

Are you sure you guys don't want any help with
anything?

KEVIN

Nope, we're good. My mom is actually really
excited about cooking for someone other than
me or herself, lol. She said she hasn't hosted
dinner guests in so long and hopes she still
knows how to carry a conversation

SARAH

My parents love her, so that won't be a problem.

KEVIN

Exactly. She worries for nothing

SARAH

And I did, too. I get that now...

I'm really sorry about not telling you right away. I
really wish I wasn't leaving early at all.

KEVIN

Let's not talk about it like this. We can take a
minute together before dinner starts

That felt like forever to wait with this apology on my chest,
but I owed him to make it when he was ready to hear it, just like
my mom said.

SARAH

Okay. I can do that

KEVIN

Thanks. See you later tonight

KEVIN

17

SARAH AND HER PARENTS WOULD ARRIVE ANY MINUTE. I GOT A FEW boxes of string lights from the Dollar Tree when my mom stopped for a few decorative items. I hung them out front on the porch, and I couldn't stop picturing Sarah's reaction to them. Would she love them as much as I thought, or was she so used to seeing them by now that she wouldn't really care? I would soon find out.

I plugged the last strand together and wound it around the last pillar. When I returned to the outlet, I plugged in the whole thing to see what I'd done.

The porch came to flashy life, blinking colored bulbs, sending their different hues against the other surfaces of the porch. I smiled because I instantly knew Sarah was going to love it. There was no being indifferent to Christmas lights, even if you'd seen millions of them. And these, I'd specifically put up just for her.

My mom came through the door, carrying the new welcome mat she'd found at the store, featuring the Nativity scene. She placed it down and straightened it out.

"I like that."

"Thanks. Me, too." She straightened out and looked around. "This looks beautiful, Kevin! Good choice picking up those lights earlier." She watched me silently accept her approval. "Sarah will love them," she added.

"I was just thinking that same thing. Also, they'll be here any minute," I confirmed by checking my watch. "Do you need me to do anything else in there?"

"Nope, everything is cooking, and will be ready not long after they arrive, the table is set, and I already set the new decorations out."

We walked inside as we talked, and I sat on the loveseat. Sighing, I relaxed into the cushions.

"Why don't you just take a minute and relax there? You seem like something's bothering you."

"Something is."

Mom closed the oven door after checking on the dinner for the hundredth time, then came to sit on the couch opposite me. "What is it?"

"Sarah and I had a little fight last night. That's why we ended up not going back up for coffee after the tree lighting ceremony."

"I thought there must've been something more than what you said. And?"

"Turns out she has to go back to school the day after Christmas to start her new job."

"Aw, baby. That really sucks for you guys. But that's good for her, congratulations. What part did you fight about?"

"She didn't tell me about it. I had no idea. I overheard her mom bring it up on the phone."

"Ah, I see. But I can see why she did that, can't you?" I looked at her in confusion. "Because you're moody."

"Excuse me?"

"Don't give me that tone. You know it's true. You can be very reactive to stuff. She probably feared that and tried to avoid it."

"It is not *my* fault that *she* lied."

"You're right, it is not your *fault* she lied. She could have just been forthright, but come on. You know you. She didn't want to upset you, and I get that. Don't judge her too harshly."

"I know, I know. And she said she didn't want to ruin the rest of our time together, I get that, but how do you simply not share something this important? I was under the impression we had another week together, but I could've been prepared for less. Some is better than none."

She shrugged. "Lying is not great, but it's a very human thing to do. We don't like to hurt those we love, and we also don't like to experience pain. I'm sure you could afford to let this one go."

"I mostly already have, but we're going to talk it out when they get here. I'll just need a minute with her. You parentals can entertain yourselves for a couple of minutes, right?"

"Boy, I ought to ground you."

"You ought to just try," I teased with a quick flick of my tongue. She rolled her eyes, but we both knew, even if I wasn't already a legal adult, she hadn't really told me what to do in years. "You're always picking on me. I figure it's the least I could do to return the favor once in a while," I chided her.

"You know I love you, but I speak the truth. You have come a long way — we both have — but don't hold this one against Sarah. It's not worth what it's taking from you. I was wondering why you two weren't together all day. Now, I know."

"I don't want to be that way," I mumbled, looking at the carpet.

"I know, and it's not your fault that you feel the way you do, but how are you going to change how you react to it?"

"I honestly don't know. I'm in a mindset where I can forgive and forget right now, but last night, I was gutted and just plain mad."

"One lost afternoon isn't the end of the world, truthfully. At least you've already grown from this experience. And you know what, I'm sure she has, too. But she still needs forgiveness as much as any of us do."

"Thanks, Mom. You're getting really good at this." I felt my face heat. I shouldn't have said that. All I did was inadvertently point out that she'd been bad at it before.

But she was thrilled by the comment. "Thanks, son. I've been trying, so I'm happy to know you're seeing a difference."

"That's a relief. I got scared for a minute that you might try to ground me again for sassing you."

"That just might happen tonight, but not over that. Change is good, and I'm satisfied to take it as a compliment."

Right on time, we heard the Stevensons pull up. Three doors opened and closed and there was chatter. Sarah's exclamation was loudest of all as she took in the lights on the porch. My mom and I shared a smile, and I hopped up, suddenly full of new vigor, and ready to make amends with my girl.

I swung open the door the second I heard feet hit the planks. Marie was right behind me.

"Hello, everyone! Come on in," she greeted them. Jonathan and Lynne were beaming, him carrying a bouquet of flowers and her holding a wrapped gift.

"These are for you, Marie," Jonathan said as he collected the present from his wife and handed both items to my mom.

My mom placed her hand over her heart before setting them on the counter. "Y'all didn't have to do this."

"Merry Christmas, Marie," Lynne emphasized with a big hug, which Mom returned.

While they were distracted having their own small talk, I pulled Sarah by the hand and nodded toward the front. Quietly, she followed me, and I closed the door softly behind her.

"Let's sit down for a minute." I gestured toward the bench.

"Your porch looks amazing, by the way," Sarah said as we got comfortable.

"I'm glad you think so."

"Are you still mad at me?" Sarah asked.

I put my arm around her shoulders. "No, I'm not mad anymore, and I'm sorry. My mom says I can be *'moody'*. Would you say that's true?"

My question seemed to throw her and, eventually, she laughed. I could see her breath mixing with the cold December air. "Maybe just a little."

"I'm sorry about that, too. If I were more easygoing and better at communicating, maybe you would have felt more comfortable telling me about the job right away."

"It's really not your fault I didn't tell you. I assumed we would fight, and we did, but not for the reason I expected."

I squeezed her hand. "How about we just accept it and move on now? Enjoy this Christmas feast Marie has put together?" I smiled. My mom was ready to shine.

"There won't be any cinnamon snickerdoodle cookies for dessert, will there?"

"Maybe." She groaned. "But they're from H-E-B." I laughed. "Come on, let's go enjoy dinner."

18

#8 JOINT FAMILY DINNER

Clearing the air with Kevin after the long day made a world of difference. I was a little on edge anticipating that conversation all day, but I'd had a lot of time to think about it and pray and come to an understanding with myself. I should have told him right away, and next time I would. Anytime something came up that affected us both would be discussed openly, period. It was the only way to survive in a relationship, especially one that was long-distance.

Kevin pulled out my chair when we returned to the group, and my mom took notice, giving me a knowing wink. I smiled in return and then listened, hoping to catch up.

"Can you believe what a talented artist you have here, Marie?" Jonathan flicked his fork at Kevin between bites. My heart swelled, so happy for him.

Marie's did, too, because her eyes were immediately shining. "Isn't he incredible? You know, I saw that talent very early on, actually. I still have a Kevin Sloan original somewhere."

Kevin grumbled. "Is it done in crayon or fingerpaint?"

"You laugh, but can you imagine how many drawings the average kindergarten teacher sees years after year? Yours was highly impressed by you."

There was no stopping me. "You don't know where that Kevin original is right now, do you?" Kevin shot me a look, and then he pressed his forehead against his hand.

Marie dabbed her mouth with her napkin, then threw it down on the table. "Of course, I do. Excuse me a moment, everyone."

"Oh, no," he moaned. "Now she's going to dig out the shoebox."

"You have no idea what you've just done," Kevin directed at me.

"I hope there are baby pictures in that box." I snickered.

"Oh, there are."

"Delightful," I clapped.

My parents were making their most polite effort to suppress their laughter, but all they did was smile behind their hands. Even my dad made an honest attempt. He must have felt bad for getting Marie going in the first place, even though it was me who asked for more.

And I regretted nothing.

I put my hand on Kevin's shoulder and patted as Marie meandered back to the table.

"All right, folks. Here we have everything from birth to second grade. Around third, I wasn't keeping track of things as much."

I sat up in my seat eagerly.

"First things first, Sarah. That drawing." She lifted the lid and sifted through it. The shoebox was more like a boot box because it was double the size of normal shoes. No wonder it could fit so many school years' worth of gems.

"Here it is." Marie delicately unfolded the picture in question, and I could hardly believe my eyes when I saw it.

"Kevin's eagle," I exclaimed reverently.

"Yep. This here is the first one I ever saw him make."

"It's terrible," came Kevin's embarrassed timbre.

"Nonsense, son. It's better than any other five-year-old out there."

Marie handed it to me for a closer look, and I ran the pads of my fingers over the waxy buildup of the blue crayon he used to create it. Down to his monotone preferences, this was every bit Kevin's eagle as the one he'd just painted at church. Just like the one from his sketchbook when we first met. God was there, working in his life all this time. Giving him a muse, trying to remind Kevin of Himself.

"It's beautiful." I turned to Kevin, and he met my gaze. "It's beautiful," I repeated, hoping this time he truly heard me.

"Thank you," he mouthed, just for me. Then to the others, "I suppose we should frame this and get it up on eBay ASAP, don't you think, Mom?"

"What are you talking about?"

"It's got to be worth money since I'm such a prodigy."

"Boy, you'll have to pry this box of treasures from my cold, dead hands. Sorry, you've gotta wait."

Laughter resounded around the table.

My mom appreciated seeing his art, too. "That really is impressive for one so young, Kevin. Thank you for letting her share it with us."

"He couldn't have stopped me," Marie casually added. "Now, I recall someone asking for baby photos, too. Am I correct?"

"I don't think — " Kevin began.

"Yes!" I finished, overjoyed with the good night.

19

AFTER UNVEILING THE MURAL AT CHURCH, ALAN FITZPATRICK called me. He'd seen the painting, and he informed me how well done he thought it was. He said my devotion to the piece came through in the brush strokes, and he wanted to know if I could put some of that dedication into a window decoration for his pet shop.

"I've never done anything like the mural before, so I've never painted any storefront windows either. I'm sure you could probably find better, someone with experience," I'd told him bluntly.

Part of me was still unused to the attention and unsure how to accept the praise. The youth room wall didn't come out half bad at all, but I was no professional.

"That doesn't matter at all. As long as you can do something pleasing with it like you did at the church, I will be happy, and so will my customers. If you could just make it animal or pet-supply-related, that would be great. We usually include a cross or something as well, but there's no need to put Christmas decor."

"I don't know. I don't have a lot of free time at the moment."

"I understand. I know I'm asking a lot. But in addition to all supplies paid for, plus a flat fee for your time, I will offer you a special discount on anything currently in the store. That's not so bad for just a couple hours of work, don't 'cha think? Plus, word travels fast around here. This one window can turn into many more. Maybe it can be the start of a new business for you."

His offer proved too good. My mouth opened as I prepared to decline again, but then I snapped it shut. What kind of fool would I be if I passed up easy cash like this? Easy cash that would not get me into trouble, but would further my artistic experience? Maybe God wanted me to do more of this. Maybe that's why it was working out so well. The opportunities were finding *me*.

And what was that he said? Anything in the store, huh?

Instead of refusing, I agreed to paint Mr. Fitzpatrick's pet shop window that same afternoon.

And he was right. It took me just under two hours, and the whole storefront was painted. I didn't even try a sketch this time, I just did something fun and festive that had been in my head.

When Mr. Fitzpatrick came out to see it, he nodded in amusement. "Kevin, you've knocked it out of the park. Again. This is magnificent, and it's only a window."

"Thank you, sir."

"I think I'll bring you back out for the next one if you're up for it."

At the rate he was paying, I definitely was. At least as long as I was home. School would take precedence, hopefully sooner rather than later. But I said I'd love to, and we shook hands again.

"Have you had a chance to look around inside? Did anything catch your eye?"

Something had, in fact. We went inside to take a closer look, and after deliberating about the discount and payment for my services, I walked away with a very exciting Christmas present for Sarah.

83

KEVIN

20

Sarah's sly look filled me with intrigue. "We can do two items at once, can't we?"

"I don't see why not." There were only two left, and tonight was the Christmas Eve service.

"Good. Then come with me." Sarah grinned widely, pulling me along. We approached the double doors to the youth sanctuary, and she turned toward me as she backed them open. "May I present to you item number nine."

Sarah's face was bright as she stood in delight over her presentation. Her arms were folded girlishly behind her back and her strawberry blonde hair was pulled over her shoulder in a loose braid. Her new bangs, which I had grown to adore, were swept to the side and pinned behind her ear. Behind her was a beautiful, live pine tree. It was at least eight feet tall, with proud, pillowy branches, thick and green.

Together, they were a wonder worth smiling over.

"I convinced Tyler to let us do this. What do you think?" asked Sarah.

"That ain't no Charlie Brown tree." Her nose crinkled as she giggled. "But I would still love it, even if it were, for the record."

"Me too."

"I've never decorated a Christmas tree before. That's why I put it on the list, so my first one would be with you."

"That's why I wanted it to be a big and full tree, with lots of room for tons of lights and ornaments. I brought my family's box of decorations with me, so they can be yours now, too. We can use anything in it you want."

I spied the box to the side of her and nodded. "You've thought of everything."

"Tyler's only request is that you put your Kevin spin on it, so the youth room continues to be the coolest in the church," Sarah tittered.

"I'm sure I can handle that."

She stepped in and slung her arms around me, pressing her cheek to my chest. "Merry Christmas, Kevin. I'm so happy I have you in my life. I don't care if I have to go back to school early. What's a few lost days, when I believe we have forever to look forward to?"

Forever.

I squeezed her back, pressing kisses into her hair. "About that... I have something for you, Sarah." I stood back, and she watched me with her tender hazel eyes, curious.

Digging into my pocket, I fished out a folded piece of paper, just like before. This time when I handed it to her, I wasn't so nervous. This, I *knew*, she would love.

Sarah opened it, and I watched as she read it, her eyes

twitching with understanding. "Kevin, this is a lease for an apartment."

"Yep."

"In Killeen."

"I know."

"With a move-in date of…" Her jaw dropped. "February first of next year?!"

"Uh-huh."

"What happened?!"

Her face was struck with surprise and I couldn't stand to draw it out any longer. "It's kind of a long story. Before the break, I applied early for the spring semester, and I was accepted."

I had to take a moment to celebrate saying that out loud. Telling the most important person in my life my good news.

"I didn't want to tell you until I had all the logistics figured out because, for a while there, I wasn't sure where the money was going to come from. Ruben — you remember my probation officer? — actually helped me apply to literally everything in the state and then some, so I got what scholarships I could. Financial aid qualified me for the rest of tuition.

"But then I had to figure out where I was going to live. Campus housing was out of the question because I didn't get covered for it, and it's too expensive for me."

I took another deep breath.

"And then, as an answered prayer I hadn't seen coming, my old buddy Merrick Serrano and I reconnected a couple of months ago. That reconnection began at the fundraiser actually, and it turns out he's up there at A&M now, renting a small house and in need of a roommate."

Sarah continued to watch me in wide-eyed astonishment, the corners of her mouth hitching up. I smiled and kept going.

"I wanted to have all my ducks in a row before I told you everything. I wanted it to be my real Christmas gift to you. It's my way of promising you forever until you let me get on my knee."

A teary-eyed laugh escaped her.

"Unless you've finally changed your mind about waiting," I quickly added, pretending like I was reaching into my coat pocket for something small and precious. She laughed and batted my hand. "So, yeah. Merry Christmas, Sarah."

"Congratulations, Mr. Sloan, official college student. I'm beyond happy for you!" Her arms flung up around my neck and I squeezed until her toes left the ground.

"Thank you."

"How did it all finally come together?"

"Merrick offered to help me get a job. They're hiring where he works and, apparently, it's better than the average student's pay. Enough to even out the rest of what I'll owe for rent and other living expenses. I lined up a few more window gigs, and my mom is going to help here and there. She won't let me refuse it. I'm going to be busy, but it'll be worth it. Plus, you know, I gotta save for a ring," I smirked.

She returned my look. "Yes, you do."

"You ready to show me how this is done?" I tipped my head toward the giant waiting tree.

"Let's do it."

When the tree was properly furnished, we stood back to admire our work.

"It's beautiful, isn't it?"

I threaded my hand with hers. "Yes, it is. Thank you for doing this with me."

"Anytime. Or at least once a year," she chuckled.

Service would start soon. We could hear the commotion of everyone arriving through the walls as we headed toward the doors. There was just one more thing I had to share.

"Oh yeah. You should know, I was able to get you something after all. Something... tangible. It's been extra difficult to keep it to myself."

"I'm not sure I can take another surprise right now. And you're supposed to be saving your money for school!" she chastised.

"Don't worry. I didn't spend a dime. I bartered part of my earnings from the window mural."

Understanding followed by excitement flooded her features. "The window mural at the pet shop?"

"Yep."

"Kevin… does my present have a heartbeat?"

"You'll get nothing out of me." I locked my lips closed with my finger and threw the imaginary key over my shoulder.

"When do I get to open this present?"

"Christmas morning. As soon as you're done with your parents, I'll be right over."

"Aw, can't I have it early?" I shook my head. "Please, please, please, please, please?"

"It's just one more night!" She dropped her shoulders and chin. Her lip was curled under in a futile but charming pout. "It'll be worth the wait, I promise."

SARAH

21

STOCKINGS WERE EMPTIED, PRESENTS WERE OPENED, THANKS WERE shared, and even more hot chocolate was consumed. It might just be my favorite winter beverage from now on. I had even taken a liking to having tiny marshmallows in it.

The fireplace was blazing, and *A Charlie Brown Christmas* was playing on the TV. Kevin was on his way and would soon arrive. It all felt just right.

And then there was the debate of Kevin's mystery gift. My dad wasn't thrilled about my assumption that it was an animal of some kind.

For a man who was sitting in elf pajamas, stirring hot chocolate, he came across as surprisingly intimidating. "What do you mean, Kevin got you a pet for Christmas?"

"I won't know for sure until he gets here, but I'm ninety-nine percent sure that's what he did. It has something to do with the window he painted at the pet shop."

"Sounds like a pretty serious gift," came my father's dramatic assessment.

"I'm sure it's not an engagement turtle or something, Dad," I teased. "Relax. It's just a present. I know it'll work out, whatever it is. Kevin is a smart guy."

"But we aren't pet people, Sarah, you know that," he said, further outing himself as the Grinch he was.

"I do know that, but I might be. What kid doesn't want a pet?"

"Non-service animals aren't allowed in your dorm. What are you going to do with it then?"

"I believe fish are allowed, Jonathan," commented my mom as she wadded up the wrapping paper from the floor.

He turned back to me. "Did Kevin get you a fish?"

If he didn't, he must have a plan. I couldn't imagine my parents wanting to pet-sit for me eight months of the year. "You'll know when I do." There was still a chance it wasn't a pet at all, and he'd been toying with me all that time, but I doubted it.

Whatever it was, I was going to love it.

Kevin's truck finally rumbled near, and I jumped up. "Yay!"

I ran to the tree and grabbed the last unopened present, hiding it under my shirt, tucked into my waistband. Then I donned my new pink bunny slippers, tossed my dad's recliner throw around my shoulders, and shuffled out to the driveway.

"Merry Christmas morning!" Kevin's window was down, but I still had to shout over the rumble of the engine.

He admiringly observed my attire. "Merry Christmas morning to you, too. Are those pink bunnies I spy down there?"

I stuck one foot out to model it. "It's only the highest of fashion for me. Don't you love them?"

"I sure do. I might need a blue pair to match." Shutting the truck off and rolling up the window, Kevin stepped out.

"If you're serious, that could be arranged."

With the blanket corners in my hands, I wrapped my arms

around him. When I backed up, I tried to peek around him, but I couldn't see anything.

"Okay, I'm ready. Where is it?"

"Where is what?"

"Kevin!"

"Oh, are you wanting your gift already?"

"Yes, please!"

Chuckling, he stepped back to open the rear driver-side door. "Close your eyes first." He waited for me to surrender with his hand on the handle.

I did so right away, squeezing them extra tight for good measure. Everything around me went still as excitement took over. Birds were chirping sweetly while the wind gently whipped around us, rustling the branches of the trees in the yard and the dried-up leaves on the ground. I shook with a slight chill.

The truck door closed. "You can look now."

Springing my eyes open, I saw Kevin holding a cage from a brass handle at the top. It was draped with a white cloth cover. When he lifted it up, there were two birds huddled together in the middle.

"Birds!" They had been the ones chirping.

"They're lovebirds. The male is a sea-green variety, and the female is a pied violet. He reminded me of the ocean, and she reminded me of you."

"Me? How?"

"She's unique and beautiful."

My eyes stung. "Put the cage down."

"Why?"

"So I don't knock it over when I hug you."

He laughed, leaning the cage against the wheel of the truck a short distance away, and I threw myself at him. He held me with my legs in place around him, rocking back and forth.

"I just learned they don't allow pets on campus, by the way," I said, my cheek resting on his shoulder.

"I know. That's why they will stay with me."

"Really?"

"Yep. It's already been arranged."

"Everything is really working out, isn't it?"

"Right now, it is. Doesn't mean it always will."

"But it will always be okay, right?"

"One way or another."

I gave him an excited kiss. "Let's go in and show my parents. My dad will be so thrilled."

"He will?"

"That they're staying with you, yes." I slid down to my feet and something stuck me in the back. "Oh, I almost forgot! Kevin, I have a gift for you as well." I reached inside the waistband of my pajama bottoms and handed him a wrapped, flat rectangle. Taking it, he looked surprised.

"Hmmm." He shook it jokingly, knowing there was no room for anything to make any noise. His gift had heart, but no beat.

"I know. Just open it."

He peeled back the sparkly silver paper, and I watched his eyes as he uncovered what it was. Slipping the gift out of an envelope, his jaw dropped. "Custom license plates?" The background was solid black with a white Texas star, and it read **SOAR**.

"I guess it's more for the Yota than you, huh?"

"This is awesome! I've always wanted something like this. I couldn't have come up with anything better to put on it, either. Thank you!"

"You're so welcome," I reciprocated, feeling the flutter of happiness in my chest.

"You're so welcome," I reciprocated, feeling the flutter of happiness in my chest.

KEVIN

22

#11. Mistletoe

My mom joined us at Sarah's house, and we all spent the afternoon together. After dinner, when it was my turn to leave, Sarah reached for my arm. "Wait a second. There's one last thing we need to do that isn't on our list."

"Oh? A number eleven?"

"We can call it that." Sarah bit her lip, and my gaze traveled upwards, following the direction of her pointed finger. A delicate, fresh bundle of mistletoe hung above her, tied together with a thin red ribbon. "Have you ever kissed anyone underneath mistletoe before?"

"Nope. Never."

"Good. I can't think of a better way to finish out our list."

Stepping under the parcel with her, I happily pulled her into my arms. From the other room, I could hear the melodious song of her lovebirds, providing us a sweet soundtrack. "Merry Christmas, Sarah."

"Cheers to our first Noel, Kevin. The first of many we'll have together."

I leaned closer until our lips brushed together. "I'll kiss to that."

Thank you for reading!

I hope you enjoyed another adventure with Kevin and Sarah. May your Christmas seasons always be Merry and Bright.

Be sure to never miss an update to the Renewed Hearts series by subscribing to my newsletter. Visit HeatherCamacho.com to get started.

God bless & happy reading!

- HEATHER CAMACHO

ACKNOWLEDGMENTS

Once again, thank You, **GOD**.

This has been a difficult year for writing. After the release of *From Graves to Gardens*, I was stuck in a frustrating place, struggling to figure out Book Two, and starting to feel like a failure. It seemed like the story wasn't taking shape properly, like my prayers weren't being answered. Turned out, I was being led to work on more Kevin and Sarah, first.

But as you read this, I am hard at work again on Book Two, and can't wait to release it in 2025. The words are flowing and the pages are turning because God is so good!

Thank you to my husband, who after 11 years of marriage is still my real life book-boyfriend, for all the sacrifices you've made for our family. I see you, I love you, and you're welcome. For what you may ask? Well, take your pick. I have many awesome qualities.

To my beta readers, Alyssa, Lando, Mom, Philip, Summer, Missy: My bad… What more can I say after telling you it'll only take an hour to read? Seriously, all of you rock. I could not have done it without you guys.

Mary Jane, you wonderful human being, you. What an incredible mother, talented author, clever decorator, and invaluable friend you are. I'm so grateful to have you in my corner!

LOVE YOU ALL & GOD BLESS — HEATHER

ABOUT THE AUTHOR

HEATHER CAMACHO'S mission is to tell stories of love and faith, dedicating her craft to sharing the testimonies, truths, and promises of the Word with readers worldwide.

A Midwesterner turned Texan, she resides on a small ranch in the southern coastal region with her husband, three kids, and their many animals.

When she isn't writing, reading, or homeschooling, she enjoys sewing clothes for her children, making quilts for her friends and spending time with her horses.

WWW.HEATHERCAMACHO.COM

facebook.com/HeatherCamachoAuthor

instagram.com/heather.author

threads.net/@heather.author

amazon.com/author/heathercamacho

goodreads.com/heathercamacho

tiktok.com/@heather.author